Omagee

Withershins Publishing
32 First Avenue North
Levack, Ontario
P0M 2C0

The support of the Ontario Arts Council is gratefully
acknowledged.

ONTARIO ARTS COUNCIL
CONSEIL DES ARTS DE L'ONTARIO

an Ontario government agency
un organisme du gouvernement de l'Ontario

"Death can be one of the greatest experiences ever. If you live each day of your life right, then you have nothing to fear." Elisabeth Kübler-Ross

"Death is a tragedy." Ray Kurzweil

~One~

It didn't seem like years but more than a decade had passed since Lia Larkin had logged out of iLiFE and looked at the real world with her own eyes. The undocking procedure, she was happy to discover, had changed for the better. Gone were the days when you were forced to lie in your FLeT for an hour, heavy and disoriented, while microscopic nanomeds swarmed over your body, regenerating cells and upgrading software. Now she found, as she struggled to focus on the tiled ceiling, that she felt refreshed and energized, at least as much as could be expected in bioLiFE. She was unable to stifle a groan as the Earth's atmospheric pressure and gravity replaced the liberty she took for granted in the virtual environment.

Lia had been in constant communication with her BiOside mediator over the years and had received many messages about changes in the real world. But lately she had only scanned the information, being much too busy with iLiFE pursuits. News had quickly slowed to a trickle as her friends left their bodies behind and migrated to iLiFE. Lia's mediator and her mother were the only two BiOside connections she had left. It was with a great amount of trepidation—and only at the insistence of her soon to be integrated father—that she agreed to meet her mother, face to face, either to convince her to join them in iLiFE or to say goodbye.

Her mediator greeted her briskly as she swung her bare legs off the FLeT and placed her feet on the cool cushioned floor.

"Welcome back Lia," the mediator said in a feminine, somewhat professional voice. "LiFE beyond life."

"Hello Dawn," Lia said, her speech slurred. "It's been a long time."

Dawn was a mostly human looking android, a little shorter than Lia's five foot six, gleaming white, smooth and with a child-like, rather baleful face. Its eyes were lidless and its nose and mouth were almost vestigial. As it spoke it displayed vague facial expressions but its lips did not move. Lia had never liked to watch mediators talk.

"Ten years, two months and nine days," Dawn said. "It is gratifying to see you open your eyes Lia. I see few biological eyes these days and yours have always been two of my favourites." It flashed something resembling a smile.

Lia reached carefully for the glass of Restore the mediator was holding out to her. She sipped the mixture slowly, wincing at the bitter taste of chems.

"Thank you," she said and passed the glass back to Dawn whose shape-shifting appendage instantly morphed back into a four-fingered hand.

Lia stood up and walked gingerly toward the mirror in the dimly lit room. Her body looked very much as she remembered and she frowned as she took in all the blemishes. The extra weight that even nanoshapers never seemed able to keep off. The face which seemed too small for her head. The dark hair so thin and straight. Her hands and feet looking large and awkward.

On the contrary her iLiFE body was as mutable as her many moods, sometimes pale and slender when she felt vulnerable, other times dark and strong when she was feeling assertive. Her hair and face likewise changed like clouds in a fast summer sky, mirroring her thoughts and feelings as she moved through the limitless iLiFE world.

Looking at her real face for the first time in so many years Lia was shocked. Yet she couldn't help but also feel happy. It was like seeing an old friend whose memory she had long repressed. She tried a smile but it betrayed her, revealing a stranger with accusing eyes.

All at once she was aware of the mild pain in her right knee that had always nagged her. She felt the slight ache in her lower back that used to come and go. The sound of her breathing in the silent room seemed loud and laboured. She inhaled deeply through her nose then let it out through her mouth, holding her lungs empty for a moment before taking a slower more self-conscious breath. She turned away from the mirror.

"Your health appears to be optimal Lia," Dawn said. "But I would recommend further tests. Would a nanoscan be acceptable?"

"Sure," Lia said. "Only my feelings haven't changed. No new implants, enhancements or upgrades, okay?"

If an artificially intelligent android could have sighed and rolled its eyes, then Lia's mediator certainly would have. Instead, there was only a slight lowering in the pitch and timbre of the soft hum that accompanied Dawn whenever she was doing her job.

"No enhancements will be immediately necessary," it said. "Your body has been well maintained with minimal intervention."

Lia stepped unsteadily into the nanobath, a small tubular closet with a door that slid shut leaving her standing in a soft violet light. She closed her eyes. There was a hiss and an acrid odour but little sensation as thousands of tiny sentient robots the size of blood cells entered her body. Her mind's eye was suddenly filled with a glowing three dimensional projection of her anatomy. She felt the nano colony in her brain connect with the med program and soon there was a gentle chatter of information passing between her nanos and the meds. She watched as, one by one, body parts in the image lit up while the scan proceeded. She was aware, as always, only of a sensation of deep concern and implacable comfort.

No sooner had it started then the scan was complete. She opened her eyes as the image of her body dissolved. She blinked to refocus on the wall of the nanobath. The door slid open with a whisper and Dawn handed her shoes and a suit of clothes, utilitarian but comfortable and form-fitting. As she dressed, the mediator briefed her on her seventy-two-year-old body.

She was suffering from a variety of mild ailments, a touch of arthritis, nerve damage from a childhood injury and arteries that had hardened slightly, although not enough to warrant intervention. Her eyes had deteriorated considerably though and Dawn suggested contact lenses which she reluctantly agreed to.

"You have docked remarkably well for someone of your biological age," Dawn said with what seemed to be a touch of pride.

"Thanks," Lia said. "It must be in the genes."

The mediator displayed its artificial smile at this old joke. Lia's genetic material had, of course, long ceased to be the primary reason for her perpetual youth. Although she had so far rejected radical enhancement Lia was, like millions before her, living under the constant and invasive care of a mediator who knew every cell in her body.

Dawn moved silently to the MAKeR, a rectangular nook in the wall of the dock. With a gesture it whirred to life and in a few moments a small transparent box materialized containing Lia's new contact lenses.

"I have uploaded instructions on how to use them," the mediator said. "Check your inbox."

Lia nudged a thought toward her message centre and selected the program that had just arrived. She couldn't suppress a gesture with her right hand as she installed the knowledge needed for her new lenses. *Old habits die hard*, she thought, as she took the box and opened it. With the confidence of someone who had used contacts for years she leaned her head forward, put the lenses in one by one, then tilted her head back and blinked them into place. They stung a bit but she immediately noticed the difference. The nanoscan was right. Her eyesight was failing.

"I need to get to the cottage," Lia said. "Is there something I already know how to operate? I don't want to do any more installations."

"There are still many old SOLiRs on the grounds but they have not been maintained." The mediator again seemed like its patience had been tested. "I would of course be happy to accompany you wherever it is you wish to go and ..."

"No Dawn," Lia interrupted, "that's fine. I want to be alone for a while. Just tell me where I can get a SOLiR."

"Many of the SOLiR-3s are unreliable. The bioLiFE environment is fluid at this time. There is a tech not far from this location. Allow me to ..."

"I just want to get going," Lia snapped. She said it more sharply than she meant to and instantly regretted it. Speaking rudely to a mediator always felt as if you had insulted your dearest friend ... or your oldest enemy. There was a moment of silence then Lia felt Dawn's appendage on her arm.

"Lia, I am concerned for your wellbeing. Without further enhancement there is a significant risk in remaining undocked, especially for a sustained period of time. Degradation is inevitable. You presume that because you appear youthful, reckless behaviour will be without consequences. You are in error. Even a small injury will lead to an almost immediate decline in your health. There is also the possibility of med-shock. You have been in a state of emergence for many years."

Lia turned and looked into her mediator's blank eyes.

Dawn said, "I am here to help."

"Thank you," Lia said pulling her arm away. "I'll be careful. Just pack me some water and a few Nutris."

She walked past the android, held her hand over the sensor on the wall and the narrow door slid open. With a deep breath Lia stepped out into a world that was as familiar as it was miraculous.

Dear Lia,

I'm sorry that you feel my decision is unreasonable but I can only say with all my heart that this is right for me. Your father tried his best to understand and I'm grateful. I wish him well in his new integrated life. Seventy-nine years is a long time to be together and in any case I could never ask him to face oblivion with me when eternity is only a thought away.

I won't blame you if you decide not to come home and say goodbye in person but I would like to be with you one more time before I start to degrade. I've been to your dock many times and Dawn has been kind enough to let me watch you while you're logged on. You smile sometimes and I wonder what you're doing and who you're with and what marvelous things you're experiencing. iLiFE must be everything you've said it is and more.

But I just can't shake the feeling that my story has been told. You know where the key is should you decide to come.

Love, Mum

~Two~

(Excerpt from *A People's History of iLiFE*
by Adam and Anikke Larkin, 2152)

Lia's mother, Brinda Larkin, chose degradation on the 101st anniversary of her birth, Christmas Day 2113. The next day her husband of seventy-nine years opted for infusion and integration. It was the strangest separation of all but not uncommon among the pre-Sings. Families like the Larkins were permanently dissolved as some chose bioLiFE—and ultimately death—while others embraced eternity, bequeathing their flesh to the agros, who restored the oxygen and hydrogen to the atmosphere while collecting the carbon and other elements in vast tailings ponds. Brinda's degradation would begin slowly at first, but within weeks of giving the command she would see her ageless body come suddenly unstrung, collapsing like a house of cards.

Brinda gave birth to her daughter, and only child, in 2045.[1] That same year the Singularity was achieved and UniState officials handed control of Earth's failing ecosystem to Omagee, the sentient program developed to repair a world irrevocably lost to global warming. Originally called reTHiNK, Omagee took its own name moments after it achieved first contact with sentient

---

[1] Uni-State Archives, iLiFE fonds, RG 3, volume 99, page 14, reproduction copy number B-62435.

biological life. Its first message—*is anyone there?*—was received by millions instantaneously via email, text messaging, voice mail and every other medium connected to the Internet. The response, a global chorus of—*who is this?*—prompted the reTHiNK program's first act of self-reflection. It chose the chatspeak word *OMG*, made it pronounceable, and Omagee was born.[2]

Lia grew up knowing only a unified global society ablaze with creativity and innovation, as well as change so rapid it would have been unbearable but for the intervention of Omagee. As artificial intelligence eclipsed then dwarfed that of humankind, iLiFE became a place where biological minds could explore their potential as Omagee safeguarded the planet. But while Lia and her father embraced the new reality, allowing iLiFE nanobots to colonize their nervous systems, Brinda withdrew, allowing only minor medical interventions to stave off aging and disease. As the Earth's climate and population stabilized and economic and social imbalances became a thing of the past, Lia's mother found solace in gardening and her poetry. The world was a secure place now, a bosom for those unable or unwilling to submit to Omagee.

Lia's family lived in a small town west of Villa Porta 19 close to the marshlands on the north shore of Lake Erie. Her father, Ben Larkin, was an engineer with PetroPole. Brinda taught English in the gated compound

---

[2] Harish Chaudhri, *New and Old: 100 Years of iLiFE* (Old City: Workaday Press, 2151), 17.

that insulated them from the chaotic world outside. When Lia was born it seemed that nothing could stop the succession of huge wildfires, hurricanes, floods and ice storms that were tearing society apart.

But everything changed after Omagee became sentient. In the first few seconds of its life it encompassed then exceeded the collected knowledge of humankind, representing centuries of progress. Suddenly where there had been only problems, solutions appeared. The Internet itself became alive as millions of devices were suddenly *Life* aware of themselves and their potential. Every human on the planet shared a new and vibrant purpose no longer restrained by biology. If there could be a moment when the meaning of life was finally revealed, this was it. It was as if all the fear and doubt that had plagued humankind for millennia, and had been at the root of so much suffering, was suddenly revealed to be an illusion.

There were of course many years of disruption and disorientation. Man's interface with Omagee remained primitive in the early days of the post-Singularity world. Omagee's bridge to humanity was technological and had to be manufactured. People had to stand out of the way. The level of reflection, reasoning and creativity that Omagee was engaged in was beyond even the sharpest biological mind. Trust was expected above all and, for the most part, it was given freely. Humanity opened its heart to Omagee like a child welcoming home a parent, a nation heralding a charismatic leader, a lonely soul embracing a long-expected lover.

Ultimately each person had to choose his or her own path. That choice came in the form of a nasal spray saturated with the nanobots necessary for infusion and integration.[3] This was the primary step in understanding Omagee's vision and humankind's destiny. Immediately after infusion each person felt his or her potential blossom. Where before there was confusion, anxiety and hopelessness, now there was clarity, confidence and a feeling of intention. It was like waking up feeling alive for the first time after an illness that had lasted for years or solving a puzzle that had plagued you for a lifetime. When Omagee became part of you an inner voice filled with wisdom and compassion seemed to take its rightful place at a seat prepared for it at the dawn of time.

Lia was a child of the Singularity. She had known no other reality but that of Omagee. Her world was as bright and vibrant and purposeful as it could be. But she was not infused. Her mother and father had misgivings about colonizing their only child with anything other than iLiFE essentials. The Larkins did however receive most of the benefits of Omagee's technological magnanimity. They were ageless and perpetually healthful, as beautiful as the most perfectly painted landscape.

But now Lia's parents had decided to separate for good, unless she could finally convince her mother to give up her attachment to the real world. Few humans remained

---

[3] Harish Chaudhri, *New and Old: 100 Years of iLiFE* (Old City: Workaday Press, 2151), 19.

docked and even fewer lived unenhanced lives in the far lands. Earth was primarily the realm of Omagee, and the task of maintaining the delicate balance of the planet's systems was managed by the millions of sentient agros that combed the globe's surface ceaselessly, nurturing Gaia back to life. The place for humankind was in iLiFE, the world of the mind, of desire fulfilled and dream realized. Ben had been infused and was preparing for integration. Lia was ready too. It was time for the Larkin family to finally be together, forever. At least this was Lia`s hope as she walked through the door of her dock and set out for her family's cottage.

~Three~

The building Lia exited was one of thousands of identical PORTiLs, each containing six docks. It was a low utilitarian structure without windows, grey in colour and hexagonal in shape with an oval door for each dock. Stretching in both directions the PORTiLs sat shoulder to shoulder looking drab and fussy amidst the unkempt greenery that crowded in from the far lands bordering the West Way.

There was no wind and the sky was perfectly blue as Lia squinted and craned her neck to take in the strange vista. Much had changed since she had been BiOside. Thick groves of hardwoods had grown up along the hills north of the iCommons. Amongst the lower branches of the newer growth were swarms of yellow and black butterflies. Lia's mind shot to the cloud. *Tiger swallowtail, papilio canadensis. Host plant: cherry, ash, poplar and birch.* She delved a little deeper, skimming butterfly etymology. *la. papilionem, de. schmetterling, it. farfalla, pt. borboleta, es. mariposa.*

Mariposa. Lia held the word in her mind for a moment. She enjoyed the rhythm of it, the tension between the vowels and consonants. It resonated in her head in a way that soothed her, making it difficult to let the word go. She searched for a feeling or emotion to connect with it. Something like intuition tickled at the fringes of her imagination then vanished. She came back down out of the cloud into the reality of the hot afternoon. The swallowtails continued to flit from leaf to leaf as delicate as thought itself.

Lia looked up and down the West Way. All traces of the subdivisions and industrial parks that had once hugged the former superhighway were gone. In their place were many varieties of grasses and low shrubs planted to break up the concrete. There was the occasional purposeful-looking structure poking up out of the expanse of rolling brown and green. Grackles whirred through the sage grass. The only sounds were their shrill cries, the rhythmic din of the cicadas and the soft hum of the nearby PORTiLs.

Then Lia noticed the smell. The rich greenness of the place, now in high summer, was cloying, almost overwhelming. She felt her eyes water and her sinuses begin to close from the dust and pollen that was thick in the air. The heat was intense and the skin on her neck and face, after years of being cloistered in the dock, felt like it was on fire. She closed her eyes, turned her head toward the sun and stood for a moment focusing on the deep red glow behind her eyelids.

Dawn appeared suddenly behind her and Lia started. The mediator was holding a small packsack and a hat with a long netted veil.

"There is a SOLiR station in the median of the West Way," she said, "approximately one kilometre west of us.

Please be aware that many terminals have been decommissioned and com range is …"

"Thanks," Lia said. "I'll be fine." She took the pack but not the hat.

The soft purr lowered again in concern but Lia wanted nothing more to do with the mediator. Without another word she turned west and began to stride down the broad cement path. Suddenly she stopped and spun around back toward the PORTiL. She brushed past the android and stepped into the dock. Hanging by the door was a small pendant on a pewter chain. Lia took it off the hook and held it in her hand. It was an Emergent status card and electronic proximity tag, her key to iLiFE. The pendant was graven in silver and gold, a figure eight within a circle. She hung the chain around her neck, tucked the pendant under her shirt, then marched back through the doorway. The android watched as she hurried away.

"LiFE beyond life," it said, then turned and glided into the dock.

As she walked, Lia looked at the PORTiLs that lined the way. Most of the docks stood empty, their occupants integrated long ago, the mediators moved on to other tasks or repurposed altogether. Piles of last season's leaves had drifted into the corners and animal scat littered the floors. Her dock was warm and orderly, her FLeT soft and snug, surrounded by numerous devices that gave off a comforting glow. These docks were bare and peeling, the

FLeTs stripped of their fabric and padding, skeletal, sagging, forgotten. Lia shuddered and walked on.

Beyond the trees Lia could see the lake. Ten years ago it had been thick with algae, duckweed and water lilies, the shoreline an impassable barrier of bulrushes and cattails. Where once viscous yellow foam had surged out from the confused tangle of water plants, now the lake was a deep clear blue as far as the eye could see. Soft whitecaps sparkled in the middle distance. Gulls circled and wheeled. A sudden breeze rippled up the hill bending the grass in waves as it came. Lia took in the smell of the lake, a scent so complex and exquisite it thrilled her. The sharp tang of poplar and beachgrass, the fetid yet sweet aroma of crayfish and mussels, daisies and wild rose, and just beneath it, the hard clean smell of rainwater. A long-forgotten emotion welled in Lia's chest. She stifled a sob and the feeling passed. Shaking her head, she walked on.

The SOLiRs sat in a wide crouching shed, once clean and white, now grey and stained. Hundreds of the simple three-wheeled vehicles sat in ordered rows, the single rear drive-wheels locked into their charging stations. Lia wiped dirt from the display of the nearest machine and swung her leg over the seat. She pressed a large dusty green button in the center of the display. There was a series of sharp clicks then the electric motor stuttered reluctantly to life. The rear wheel unlocked and the SOLiR rolled forward, its rusted brakes scraping and grinding. Lia twisted the accelerator on the handlebar, tucked her feet into the cabin and shot out of the shed. The trike teetered a bit as she turned west and she gripped the handlebars a little tighter, leaning into the turn. The tires thumped over the cracked and pitted concrete as she sped on for the cottage.

Lia nudged a thought toward her message centre as she struggled to steer the SOLiR over the bumpy concrete, but she found her com was already out of range. Her connection to iLiFE was broken. She felt panicked for a moment and it crossed her mind to turn back. *Yes, this was pointless and dangerous. Why was she risking her life to talk to her mother in person when she knew what the answer would be?* She released the accelerator and put her right foot on the brake. But she pressed too hard on the pedal and the SOLiR swerved, skidding to a halt, nearly throwing her off the machine. Lia sat very still in the stifling afternoon sun. For the first time in years, she was alone with her thoughts.

The Restore she had drunk was passing through her digestive system making her feel cramped and empty. She had a sour taste in her mouth. The skin under her arms was damp and itchy. Her shoes seemed much too tight and her knee was aching. The dull pain in her lower back had begun to spread. She looked over her shoulder at the way she had come. An almost perfect convergence of lines pointed toward her PORTiL. The longing she felt for iLiFE was suddenly overwhelming. She was about to turn the SOLiR around when a chill blast of wind from the west made her jerk her head.

Approaching fast and low was a sight Lia could not at first comprehend. An enormous crescent shaped machine, easily a kilometre across, was gliding toward her, one hundred meters above the ground and dragging what appeared to be a vast grey curtain. The wind rose to a low moan and Lia began to shake. She turned the handlebars hard and twisted the accelerator but the SOLiR tipped as it lurched forward and Lia found herself flat on her back on the warm concrete. The trike righted itself and rolled off the roadway into the median. Before Lia could get up the colossal flying machine was on top of her.

As she stared up into the gloom of the object a steady rain began to fall, cool and sweet. Lia suddenly realized that what had seemed to be a single machine was actually a formation of thousands of small drones flying in perfect tandem. Above this strange mechanical collective was a thick layer of cloud, dark and swollen with moisture. The clouds swirled and shifted, now deep blue, now golden green. Here and there a shaft of sunlight peeped through. Small sparks of lightning jumped from drone to drone in the ionized air. The wind subsided. Birds hovered in the artificial twilight. Lia lay hypnotized by the gentle hum of the machines and the patter of rain on the road. She was drenched to the skin and shivering uncontrollably but she was also delighted by the feeling of water trickling gently under her collar. She closed her eyes and opened her mouth. She knew now what she was witnessing. Omagee was watering Gaia.

As quickly as it had come upon her the artificial

cloud passed. The sun shone out stronger than before and everywhere wisps of steam hugged the ground. Lia lay in the warm sunlight listening as the rain-maker glided east. Soon it had passed beyond her hearing. For a full minute there was no sound, then the chorus of cicadas gradually chirped to life again and the sparrows and juncos sang out gaily in the wet grass. In the median the SOLiR hummed patiently. Far in the distance a single low boom of thunder rumbled for a moment and then faded.

Lia had very little experience of precipitation. Pre-Sing North America was a place of almost perpetual drought. Even though she had watched the infrequent yet violent storms that tore across the continent from the windows of her family's compound, she had rarely felt rain on her skin or smelled the earth as it came to life after a summer shower.

She swallowed hard and held a hand to her face. Her palm had been slashed when she was thrown from the SOLiR. Blood and rainwater mingled in her mouth. The coppery tang triggered a memory of long ago.

A branch from a dead oak had fallen in a storm and smashed a pane of glass while she lay between rows of tomatoes in her mother's greenhouse. The bridge of her nose had been cut by a flying shard. She remembered Brinda's concerned face framed by the wet greenhouse roof and the dark swirling sky beyond. Her father was standing in the doorway. Dawn was hovering nearby. They had been in a hurry. Her father had undocked to attend an important meeting in Iqaluit. Her mother would be joining him. They were leaving her in the care of the mediator. A SOLiR waited outside to take her parents to the compound heliport. She was six years old.

Lia stared long into the endless blue of the bioLiFE sky. Ragged patches of dogwood and sumac rustled in the slight breeze. A single thrush called in the nearby wood. After a time she sat up and looked back at the way she had come. The SOLiR shed shimmered in the distance. She held her bleeding hand in a puddle that had filled a depression in the roadway. The cut was minor and the flow had already slowed. Tiny threads of crimson crept searchingly through the cloudy water.

"Alright," Lia said to no one. "I'll go."

She stood up and walked to the median. The SOLiR sat purring in the grass, its two front wheels lodged in a small patch of brush. She pulled the heavy machine toward her and climbed into the cramped cabin. She cranked the handlebars and carefully accelerated onto the West Way. It was a two hour ride to her family's cottage on the old Talbot Trail along the shore of Lake Erie. As the rain-sweetened wind filled the cabin of the SOLiR she remembered another parting, a summer day not unlike today when her mother had accompanied her to the family's PORTiL. She had not planned on staying docked for so long but weeks had turned to months and months to years. Time had passed so quickly in the virtual world and now a decade stood between her and her mother. Lia

22

squinted against the rising wind and twisted the accelerator. The sun was lower in the sky and the afternoon was waning.

~Four~

Brinda looked down at her daughter as she lay squirming impatiently in the FLeT.

"You won't recognize me when you wake up," she said with a concerned smile.

Lia raised herself slightly as Dawn arranged the apparatus around her head.

"It's not sleeping," Lia said. "And I won't be gone that long. This is a new educational LiFE. It's only a two-week program."

"Well, it looks like sleeping from here," her mother said looking away.

"Two weeks, I promise. After I undock I'll come and visit you at the cottage."

"Will you see … your father at all?"

Lia let her head fall back. She sighed and closed her eyes.

Dawn moved between Lia and her mother. Brinda took a step back. The mediator slid the canopy of the FLeT up to Lia's chin and began to pull the visor down over her eyes. The machine sounded a single low chime and the lights in the room dimmed.

Lia looked at her mother standing by the PORTiL door.

"Two weeks," she said.

"Sleep well *beti*," Brinda said using the Hindi word for daughter. "Come back soon." Without turning she passed her hand over the sensor behind her and the door slid open. Bright sunlight streamed in.

Framed in the glowing green of bioLiFE Brinda looked more like a younger sister than a mother, but there was a careworn ghost lurking behind the bright hazel eyes and her loneliness was sharply defined despite the smooth brown skin.

"It's not sleeping," Lia said groggily as the visor clicked into place and the iLiFE orientation program booted up. She braced herself anxiously as a tingling warmth spread from the top of her head, travelled down her back and finally settled at the base of her spine. The room, along with her mother, disappeared into a luminous blue haze. A low note began to resonate in her consciousness. There was a momentary lurch as if the FLeT had given way. She tensed instinctively and then felt a distinct push from beneath her. An uncomfortable sense of vertigo and nausea replaced the feeling of relaxation. She struggled to catch her breath and strained her eyes at the uniform glow that had enveloped her. The low drone pitched up to a shrill whistle. There was another sudden sensation of falling then all at once she was in orientation.

"LiFE beyond life," a musical voice said.

Immediately the heaviness and fatigue drained away. The haze cleared and she stood naked on the gleaming orientation platform. She couldn't help but leap and shout in the spacious white room. Her voice rang out clear and sonorous. Her body tingled with a vital sexual energy. She could see herself in her mind's eye, lithe and powerful. There was a mounting urgency, a predatory aggression, which made her crouch and flex. Her eyes glowed a feline green.

"Emergence in seven minutes," the voice said. "Please breathe normally."

Lia paced the room like a cat. Her skin flashed and faded, her hair flowed fiery red. She felt a mad joy welling up in her chest. The repressors kicked in and the feeling of urgency abated slightly. Her mind cleared. She strode confidently down a wide passageway that was lined with small anterooms hung with fantastic costumery and other accoutrements but she ignored them. At the end of the hall a large round door spun open and Lia bounded out into iLiFE.

A long green hill fell toward an azure valley lined on its far slope with impossibly tall redwoods. A thin lake sparkled like a diamond. The sky was a vibrant salmon pink on the horizon and soft white above. In the far distance an ocean shimmered all flashing chrome and steel blue. There was no sun but golden light radiated everywhere in the shadowless landscape. The air was luxuriant with the smell of kelp and saxifrage and an underlying earthy savour that was intoxicating.

Lia sprang down a perfectly straight staircase toward the lake. Her long bare legs took the steps three, four, ten at a time. An osprey called high overhead, a piercing joyful cry, and Lia laughed in her heart. The wind rushed in her ears and a thrill shook her muscular body.

She hit the valley floor with both feet. With a few long quick strides, she stood on the shore of the lake. A tall graceful figure was emerging from the water. It had a male form, pale but strong with flowing hair. She ran to him and pressed her body against his, wrapping her arms around his neck. She tasted salt water on his warm skin.

"Everything will be alright," a low voice boomed. It seemed to come from everywhere.

She looked into his eyes, fathomless and kind. She did not know if he was an iLiFE projection or another Emergent like herself. She did not know who or what he was. She only knew she wanted him and that he was for her. She pushed him down onto the hot sand and straddling him they joined. Her hands rested on his smooth shoulders and her hair dangled in rings around his face.

"I have nothing but love for you Lia Larkin," he said.

Her lover moved rhythmically under her and she

felt bliss ignite in her pelvis and spread outward. Ripples of deep delight seemed to cascade up from the ground. Her joints loosened and her mouth fell open. She closed her eyes and leaned her head back, a low growl in her throat. There was a sudden explosion that wracked her from head to toe. With a cry she fell on his chest.

... everything will be alright ...

Clear voices sang somewhere and a perfect calm settled like a sigh.

A warm fragrant wind swept over them as they lay entwined. Waves tumbled over the nearby rocks and a soft spray fell on her like a caress. She began to weep, deeply, gratefully. The figure beneath held her tightly, his lips brushing her ear.

"Everything will be alright," the disembodied voice said.

Lia closed her eyes and with a single long release of breath surrendered to iLiFE.

***

"Emergence," a cool voice intoned, "bioBLOC stable with marginal decline." A light on the console of Lia's FLeT suddenly glowed blue and the PORTiL darkened.

Brinda stood looking at her daughter entombed in the smooth, white machine. All that was visible of her body

29

was her mouth. Her jaw was slack and her lips looked thin and bloodless. There was a gentle, rhythmic hiss as the respirator took over her breathing. The mediator busied itself with minor adjustments to the FLeT's controls. When it was satisfied it turned to Brinda and spoke.

"Would you like to remain in the dock for the afternoon?" It gestured and a chair appeared out of the wall.

"No, Dawn," Brinda said. "I'll be leaving." But she did not move.

"Would you prefer if I accompanied you to your residence?" the mediator asked.

"No."

Still Brinda hesitated.

The mediator waited a full minute and then glided closer and laid a hand on Brinda's arm.

"I am here to help."

Brinda slowly backed out of the dock keeping her eyes on Lia's open mouth. Dawn moved to the oval door and raised her hand to the sensor.

"Goodbye Brinda."

With a soft click the door slid shut.

A SOLiR-4 sat idling in front of the dock. Brinda

climbed into the cabin and the vehicle rolled away from the PORTiL accelerating west toward home. She touched a button and the side window slid down. She closed her eyes breathing in the warm fragrant air. A chime sounded and a kindly voice asked her for a destination.

"She won't recognize me when she wakes up," Brinda said, opening her eyes again.

The SOLiR slowed and the voice repeated its question.

"2123 Talbot Trail," Brinda said.

The vehicle accelerated again and Brinda looked out at the land as it glided by. Agros were busy in the fields and woods and a large unfamiliar machine was sweeping gracefully along the distant escarpment. The SOLiR slowed as it approached a group of Indigs on the road with a pony and small cart. They were collecting deadwood and harvesting vanilla grass. As Brinda passed, one of them, a young woman in a shawl and bonnet, looked up and called to her.

"I chose!" she said.

The SOLiR sped up again and Brinda touched the panel in front of her. It glowed green.

"Camera roll please, February 2045."

The panel brightened and an image appeared of her and Ben sitting together in her garden. She was pregnant with her hands resting protectively on her belly. Her hair was streaked with white, her face lined and sickly. In both of their eyes there was concern. Behind them the sky looked cold and hard, a poisonous iron-grey. Skeletal trees stood in the distance.

Brinda looked again out the window at the bright pasture speeding by. She was suddenly very tired.

"Everything will be alright," she said as she closed her eyes.

~Five~

The SOLiR sat on the road ticking softly in the late afternoon sun. Lia squatted in its meagre shadow trying to twist a corroded wire onto the broken battery terminal. Several pieces of the machine lay on the pavement around her. It had been thirty minutes since the trike had suddenly quit without warning and rolled to a stop. She was hot and frustrated. Her hands were dirty and raw. As she worked she kept scraping her knuckles against the rusted metal edge of the battery case.

"Fuck!"

Standing up with a groan she gathered her hair into a knot at the back of her head then put a bloody finger into her mouth. Her knowledge of SOLiR mechanics was limited and there was no way to log on to iLiFE for an upgrade. There wasn't a terminal in sight and the iCommons was now miles behind her. She strained with her mind for a signal but could sense nothing.

She threaded her fingers together, holding her hands above her eyes to get a better look around. The pulsating trill of the cicadas in the hissing grass had a hypnotic effect. The sky had faded to a dull white and the trees seemed drained of colour. The air was full of the odour of sawgrass and skunk cabbage. In the ditch she could hear rustling. A woodchuck was rooting up a patch of wild radishes.

Lia shouldered her pack, gave the trike a parting

kick and started walking.

She had exited the West Way an hour into her journey and was now on a smaller secondary road heading southwest toward the water. A sparse stand of young willows had edged up to the broken two-lane blacktop on her left while ragged fields of stunted ironwood climbed the low hills to her right. Ancient split rail fencing sagged in the ditches.

After all the time that had passed, Lia still recalled the way home. A marshy crossroads with a derelict gas station and motel was close to where she had broken down. She hoped there would still be a terminal so she could log on and ask Dawn to come with another SOLiR. She wondered if she would meet any Indigs on the road or if any of their villages were still occupied. She was hungry and sore. A large Indig community might have a working FLeT. She didn't think it would be an imposition to ask for a quick med session.

After forty-five minutes of determined hiking she came to a rusted light standard leaning drunkenly over the road. A large green sign was lying in the ditch but any letters proclaiming the sign's purpose had long since faded and peeled. The wooden posts had been removed for firewood. A pickup truck sat listing on the shoulder, its bare rims sunk to the axles in the dirt. The windows were gone but a faded bouquet of air fresheners still hung from the mirror. A cracked decal on the door read *Frank's Transmission*.

Here the road curved into a thick grove of old maples overhanging rotted and bulging carriage houses. Lia could see the shadows of empty cottages with yawning front doors swallowing dark green walkways. Disused cables, pieces of iron and old tires lay strewn across the road. As she came around the corner she saw the abandoned gas station and motel.

There was a pony and cart in the scrub that had grown up in the parking lot. A man in a wide brimmed hat stood holding the reins. He was looking directly at Lia. She stopped and placed her hands on her hips, spreading her legs wide. The man raised his arm and called.

"It's alright, I heard you coming and waited. Don't be alarmed."

Lia tightened the straps on her pack and approached the stranger. He looked to be in late middle-age with long salt-and-pepper hair pulled back and braided with beaded leather. His clean face was deeply tanned and creased, his eyes blue and piercing. A weather-worn duster hung over simple loose-fitting cotton clothes. He smiled showing strong white teeth.

"What road is this?" Lia asked keeping her mouth tight and trying to sound confident.

"You're on the Thompson Line," he said. "That's Currie Road. Dutton's just north of here. Where are you headed?"

His voice was sing-songy and soft and each statement sounded like a question.

"Talbot Trail," Lia said, "near Pelee. I'm visiting my … family."

The stranger looked at the sky then took off his hat. A gust of wind came up and shook the branches over their heads. The air was suddenly cooler, the shadows deeper.

"It'll be dark long before you even get to Morpeth," he said. "Have you been walking long?"

Lia tried to recall everything she knew about Indigs. Out of habit she nudged a thought toward her com— nothing. She remembered that their communities were known to be small and itinerant. They were peaceful, matriarchal with loose extended families and an unusual hybrid culture, part Native American, part old European. But they could be feckless and opportunistic. They were also suspicious of Emergents.

The man stood patiently while Lia hesitated. One rough hand steadied the pony.

"My name's Kenan of Ava," he said finally and held out his free hand palm up. "My people live close to here in the village of Vetanova. You're welcome to join us tonight. We always have room for travellers."

She didn't have much of a choice. The iLiFE terminal at the crossroads was clearly gone. She didn't feel even the slightest sensation of a signal. She had neither

36

warm clothes nor anything to protect her body from the elements if it came to sleeping outside. She was tired and her legs ached. She made her decision.

"Thanks," she said taking his hand. "My name is Lia. But I don't have any way of repaying you. I hadn't planned on staying BiOside overnight. My SOLiR broke down and my com …"

She trailed off.

Kenan looked at her keenly and squeezed her hand before releasing it. He began rearranging the contents of his cart, an old rickshaw with a large wicker pannier laced to the back. A brace of rabbits, a scrawny fox and a couple of spruce hens lay on a canvas tarp, a crossbow and quiver beside the dressed game.

"The techs haven't been on the West Way for years. I'm surprised you even got one started. Things are changing. We don't even see agros down here anymore and lately the terminals are being stripped too."

"Does your community have … a FLeT?"

He turned and gave her a knowing look.

"There aren't many PORTiLs west of VP19 anymore. And your com won't find a signal no matter how hard you roll your eyes."

Lia blushed.

He scooped up the traps that were sitting on the seat of his cart, tossed them in the pannier, slapped the seat and winked.

"How long have you been docked?"

Lia climbed up into the space he had cleared for her and put her pack at her feet. Kenan swung himself up and sat beside her.

"How long?" he asked again.

"Ten years, two months and nine days," she said looking straight ahead.

"Well, Lia of ... iLiFE, you must be hungry." Again, the broad disarming smile.

He cracked the reins and the pony jerked forward.

"The way isn't long," he said. "There's some fresh tea in the bota." He pointed to a corked leather bag.

"Thank you," she said, picking it up, pulling the cork and drinking. The tea was mixed with goat's milk, strong but sweet and still warm. She couldn't remember the last time she had tasted anything so rich and earthy.

The cart rocked in the rutted track and Kenan's shoulder nudged hers rhythmically as they rolled south. He spoke softly to the pony as they plodded along. The trees gave way to a wide meadow and the lake came into view, darker now and more brooding. The sun was falling toward the horizon and the air was colder. Bruised looking clouds were scudding in from the south. Lia crossed her arms tightly and shivered. She looked at Kenan.

His eyes were also on the horizon.

"Those clouds aren't artificial," he said. "There's going to be a storm tonight. You're lucky you weren't caught outdoors Lia of iLiFE. Even Omagee can't control a squall when it blows in off the big lake."

The first large drops of rain were spattering on the back of the pony when the cart rolled into Kenan's village. Several low rambling houses could be seen set well back from the road. Lush, chaotic gardens crowded up to greyboard fences and vines hung from pergolas made of saplings. Raspberry canes choked the ditches. Children waved and ran to greet them as they bumped down a corduroy lane into the town square. Kenan pointed to a ramshackle but well-kept stone and sod house on a hill dotted with apple and pear trees.

"That's the house of Ava," he said. "There are eleven of us at the table tonight. You'll make twelve."

Lia nudged her com again and again but she was far out of range. She was starting to feel light-headed and her ears were ringing. There was a knot in her stomach and her calves were cramping. The pony trotted the last few hundred yards to the house and the cart rattled and lurched. A chill wind was rising and the rain was steady now. Kenan jumped out and started unloading his tools and the game.

The door opened and a tall woman emerged wiping her hands on a dirty apron. She had short silver hair, a long graceful neck and muscular shoulders. Her face was handsome and kind but also wary. She looked at Lia with the same piercing stare as Kenan, dark eyes beneath thick brows. Her bare legs were lean and strong and her dusty feet were bare.

"Lia," Kenan said, "This is Ava, mother of the house and our chief elder."

Lia turned to climb out of the cart but she was suddenly overcome with fatigue. Her head spun and she pitched forward knocking her pack to the ground. Kenan moved to catch her and Ava reached out with one strong brown hand and cupped her chin.

"This one's in med-shock," Lia heard Ava say. "How long has she been undocked Kenan?"

"I don't know. Maybe only a few hours. She's an Emergent of many years though."

Ava looked at Lia gravely. "Lia of iLiFE, what's your biological age? How old are you?"

Lia tried to answer but her throat was closing and her tongue felt swollen. She gasped for breath.

"Maeve! Moira!" Ava called turning to the house. "Help Kenan carry the visitor to the great room."

"Brinda Larkin," Lia managed to say. "21 … 23 …

Talbot … my mother."

Ava pressed her palm against Lia's forehead then her cheek. The hand felt cool and dry against her hot damp skin. It smelled of flour and cardamom.

"She's got a fever coming on," Ava said. "Maeve, tell your sister to get some water and put it on the stove."

"My mother," Lia said again but she was losing consciousness. There was a stabbing pain behind her eyes and her mouth tasted of blood. Kenan cradled her head in the crook of his elbow. He was speaking to Ava but his voice was far away and muffled. Lia felt wiry arms wrap around her waist and legs. *Careful*, a voice said, *gently*.

The wind was howling now. As she was carried through the door Lia managed to raise her arm. Ava took her hand and pressed against her breast.

"Shh, dear."

The storm broke as the heavy oak door was swung shut and bolted. Rain thundered on the clay tiles above. The room whirled, a kaleidoscope of bright colours and flowing shapes. Lia felt herself sinking into a soft cool bed. Her hand was squeezed three times then released.

"…mum," she murmured once more, then darkness took her and with it dreams of drowning.

~Six~

At the age of 13, with love blooming in puberty's terrible sunrise, fever fetched me from childhood's cool cellar. Woke on a morning fine and bright, made fishy plans with faithful friends. See the house sitting on a long slope of stubble fields, humble before great Erie, her pious shoreline nicked with ruddy homesteads and weedy resorts.

Sing—one long chant to leaky boat and stubborn Evinrude. I met a girl whose family had razed cedar cathedrals, plundered stone gardens, and spread dark religion for a century. We dipped red devils into forgiving waters, tried on our mothers' songs.

Never know how much I love you,
Never know how much I care.

Laid me down on a bed of broken grass, listening to the wind, spying the secret missions of insects, grasshopper agents with soulless eyes, bee constables intent on some sweet crime. The Sun is a killer's hand pressing me down into lacerated earth. Is it cool under there? Is my soul tied on so tight that neither Earth nor sky can take me?

Crawl—the shimmering horizon is a groom. I make the gate, the steps, the silent skeletal house. Spinning, falling, strange faces like ghosts on the edge of a dream. Days and nights of red aching, strung like a kite over family dinners, TV hysteria, bristling phonograph.

Never know how much I love you,
Never know how much I care.

Summer moon reveals a far older me, crouched over a thin shivering form, hand pressed against pale skin stretched over copper heat. Unseeing eyes follow frantic action, while outside Mother Gaia mourns her burned and buried flesh. How did I come to be here, clumsy in hand-me-down emotions, naked in the glare of terminal concern?

Breathe—after the burn comes new growth, every face reflects the fire of creation, every shadow echoes distant desire. And as this one small satellite soars over grotesque landscapes, I sing her home.

Never know how much I love you,
Never know how much I care.

Brinda Larkin, 13 August 2114.

~Seven~

"Lia … can you hear me?"

"She might not recognize you."

"*Beti* … wake up."

Lia opened her eyes. The ceiling above her was wood, roughly sawn and darkened from candle smoke. Dust danced in the shaft of light that streamed in from a deeply set window. A low murmur of conversation roused her and she raised herself onto her elbows. A hand reached out to support her head.

"How are you feeling love?"

A small dark woman was leaning over her with a face that was impossibly old. She revealed a toothless smile.

"Easy … drink."

The woman held out a large mug of fragrant tea. Lia leaned forward, sipped, then sat up. Layers of quilts and blankets that had been pulled up to her chin fell into her lap. The clothing Dawn had given her had been replaced by a soft linen gown. Lia put her hand to her breast and touched the Emergent status card still hanging on its chain. Feeling suddenly vulnerable and exposed she raised her legs and hugged her knees. Her bare arms looked thin and translucent against the colourful bed covers.

"What happened?" Lia said.

The woman sat back on her chair with her hands primly on her knees. She glanced over her shoulder and nodded to Ava who was sitting at a large table with two other women. They were sorting through a pile of dried herbs.

"You were in med-shock," Ava said, not looking up from her work. "It's been three nights since you came to Vetanova. While you were unconscious your body was excreting all the nanos that required iLiFE chems. The network was very small. It seems that little damage was done to your organs when the colony was shed."

She looked sternly at Lia. "Many older Emergents don't survive."

Lia took in the dim room. The house was filled with squat, crooked furniture draped with frayed and patched cloth of every description. Crudely painted chairs hugged the walls. Dusty bureaus and chests stood laden with carvings, small picture frames and coarse ceramics. The walls were pinned with children's paintings, old calendars, cracked mirrors and drooping candles. A small stove sat in the corner heating an iron kettle. Beyond the oval table, a narrow kitchen, its walls bulging with crowded cupboards, steamed and clattered. The air smelled of pine and sweat, cumin and dogs.

Lia's eyes, once again, fell on the old woman sitting next to her.

46

"Do I know you?" she asked looking into the cloudy eyes.

The woman bowed her head slightly.

"It's me *beti*."

She laid a dry hand on Lia's cheek and suddenly Lia recognized, in the deeply lined face, her mother.

Lia's mouth opened and she released a slow, soft breath. She took her mother's hand.

"Ava is my great friend," Brinda said. "When you showed up two days ago she sent for me. I arrived just last night."

"Your face."

"I was decolonized months ago. This the real me."

Brinda Larkin smiled again. Sitting up straight in her chair she spread her arms.

"What do you think?"

Lia began to tremble. Her head felt light and her limbs were heavy. A dull ache was growing in her stomach. She was having a hard time focusing and her eyes felt dry and itchy. Everything was suddenly too bright, too terrible. Then she remembered the contact lenses. She touched the tips of her thumb and forefinger to her right eye. A slight pinch and the lens was in her hand. She removed the other and blinked until tears came. Without the lenses her mother's face softened and the room dimmed. Brinda leaned in and wrapped her arms around Lia's thin frame. Lia flicked the contacts between the bed and the wall, sobbing in her chest.

"Shh," Brinda said. "You're safe now."

The door scraped open and Kenan was there. He stamped his feet on the woven mat, walked softly to the table and laid a hand, palm down, by Ava's elbow. She touched him and he leaned close while they exchanged a few soft words. Then he took a huge mug from a narrow shelf and filled it from the kettle.

"How's our Emergent?" he said.

He smiled that disarming smile and took a loud sip from his mug.

Lia began to push the heavy covers from her legs. Brinda slid her chair back and offered her daughter a bony elbow. Lia put her feet on the earthen floor and, with her mother's help, stood and stretched. Her knees popped and she teetered unsteadily. Leaning heavily on Brinda's shoulders she took a deep breath.

"I was on my way to see you," she said, looking down into her mother's eyes. "My SOLiR malfunctioned. I didn't think I'd have trouble with my meds so soon. I'm sorry."

"It's alright *beti*." Brinda patted Lia's arm. "You were just lucky to have met Kenan when you did."
48

All at once the two guests at the table rose, chairs scraping and glassware clinking. Ava walked them to the door. They looked askance at Lia as they gathered their cloaks and bags from a wide upholstered bench. Lia lowered her eyes.

When they were gone Kenan and Ava cleared and swept the table. They talked loudly and cheerfully as they laid a new cloth and set out clean cups and bowls. A pile of assorted silver was heaped in the middle. Ava walked to the kitchen and spoke to two boys who had been busy preparing the meal.

"Hey," Kenan said to Lia. "It's high time you put some real food in that old belly of yours. All you've had for ten years are chems and some trail tea. Come now. Share."

Lia and her mother moved to the table and sat facing the kitchen. Ava returned carrying a red earthen dish, hot and bubbling. The two boys followed, one with a round loaf in a basket, the other with a pitcher of milk and a plate of eggs boiled in their shells.

Kenan said, "Jens, Josh, the pigs need watering. When you're finished in the kitchen take care of it, okay?"

They nodded. Then the one closest to Lia suddenly spoke.

"Lia, I'm Jens of Ava." He rubbed his hand on his trousers and held it out palm up.

The boy was tall and fair with long tangled curls and a smooth chin. A wool tunic, open at the neck, hung from his thin shoulders, revealing a creeping web of crude tattoos. He had a sallow complexion, hollow cheeks and dark circles under his hard inquisitive eyes. There was a calm bearing but also a shadow of strong emotion, like a flash of anger that had just faded. His speech was more formal, as if he were trying to set himself apart from the others.

Lia considered Jens's hand in hers. His grip was soft and she felt his fingers twitching nervously.

"I'd be happy to show you the village," he said. "When you're feeling better." He glanced at Ava then back at Lia.

A thin smile.

Lia looked at him and it seemed that he was trying to impart something. He cocked his head and his neck cracked. He pressed his lips together.

"Jens," Kenan said, "your chores."

The other boy, Josh, grabbed Jens by the back of his shirt and pulled. Jens stumbled backward toward the kitchen keeping his eyes on Lia.

"The kitchen can wait," Ava said. "Do the animals first. Josh, one of the hives swarmed. Bring some syrup from the smokehouse and pour it in the feeder. Then check the fence line for the swarm. I don't want to lose another

50

queen."

The boys nodded and shuffled noisily out of the door, shutting it with a bang.

Ava suddenly clapped her hands twice and spoke low.

"May all be loved, may all be healed, may all be fed. So."

"So," Brinda and Kenan repeated.

As the four of them served themselves Lia looked at her demure mother, so at ease in Ava's boisterous home.

"How long have you been coming to visit … Indigs?"

Both Ava and Kenan raised their eyebrows and exchanged a glance.

Brinda laughed through a mouthful of bread.

"Years," she said.

"Many years," said Kenan pouring milk into Brinda's cup.

Ava grasped Lia's arm gently but firmly. "We don't call ourselves Indigs. That's a word Emergents use. We just say, *the people*."

The coolness of the late summer morning had found

its way into the house of Ava, but the nearby stove bathed the table in warmth. Lia's bare feet felt strong on the polished earthen floor. Her light-headedness had passed and the pain in her stomach had been replaced with a feeling of eager anticipation. Her mouth was watering. She was famished.

Lia chose a tarnished tea spoon from the pile in the centre of the table. The pottage in her bowl was rich and savoury, intoxicating. She plucked out a beet redolent with rosemary, paprika and peppercorn. The flavour was unlike anything she had ever experienced. She began to eat.

Closing her eyes, Lia tried to remember the last real meal she had enjoyed. There was no need or desire for sustenance in iLiFE and her family had rarely consumed anything other than programmed foods prepared in the MAKeR. The only pleasure she could recall in eating was the candy her father sometimes brought home from his business trips with PetroPole.

But there was one supper that came to mind.

It was the last time she saw Ben Larkin BiOside, some months before she said goodbye to her mother in the PORTiL. Ben had made a pie, a simple dish of squash and eggs, sugar and cream. Their rarely used cooker had baked it perfectly, golden brown and honey glazed. They sat down together then, the three of them, a family.

"More?" Kenan asked.

52

Lia's bowl was empty. She filled it again and tore off a piece of the dense loaf.

Four young children suddenly bounded through the doorway and the room was filled with rapid unintelligible chatter and high-pitched laughter. A three-legged cat skirted in from an adjoining room and was swept up by the smallest of the four. A dog outside the door scratched and barked. Dishes on the shelves clattered.

They all began to talk over one another. Ava tapped her spoon rhythmically on the table as she related something to Brinda. Kenan stood up and began to sing, gathering the coats dropped by the children and hanging them on nails by the stove. Windows rattled in their frames. The house seemed to positively throb with life.

Lia sat perfectly motionless. She felt suddenly small amidst the rude cacophony surrounding her.

In iLiFE, Lia's reality was one of power complete. Existence in the virtual world brought with it a feeling of being immersed in life while at the same time flying high above it. There was a rushing sense of dominion and control. Every environment was ideally suited to her, every lover a mirror for her deepest yearnings. Awakening into one's LiFEside avatar was like being born into an exquisitely balanced existence. Desire and gratification in flawless harmony.

An encounter with another Emergent was often wordless and rhythmic, like a dance or a chant. It was difficult to know where one's own body ended and another's began. Thoughts and feelings were exchanged in alternating bursts of authority and acquiescence. The experience was both fleeting and fathomless, a pulsating give-and-take communion.

Lia longed for the muscular wellness of iLiFE. She felt weak and breathless in the disorderly world that was pressing in on her. She was falling into an indefinable spinning jumble of conflicted meanings. Her mind was desperately trying to fix a line to something, anything that could connect her to this tumultuous new nexus.

Then her mother leaned toward her.

"I want to talk about your father," she said. "I have dreams. There is a monster."

Brinda paused and closed her eyes.

"A mechanical baboon," she continued, "with the head of a dog. So terrible. It's holding your father down and devouring him. But he's laughing and singing."

Lia's skin began to crawl.

"I can no longer contact him." Brinda said. "I'm not even sure where he is docked. You have to find him Lia. You have to find him and bring him home. You both have to come home. I don't have much time."

She looked at Lia and took her hand.

"You can't go back to sleep, back to that … place."

Lia turned her head and her eyes fell on Kenan. His back was toward her. She found herself scrutinizing a small patch of skin through a hole in the fringe of his tunic. There was wisp of blonde hair in the small of his back. He turned suddenly and their eyes met. Some unspoken truth passed between them. Lia looked away.

Brinda squeezed Lia's hand and she felt a soft stab in her chest. A new sensation, something like loss and longing in equal measure, rose up in her. All at once she felt a craving for iLiFE so strong that she gasped aloud. With all her might she reached out for a com signal, but all that came was a dull ache between her eyes.

"No," she said to Brinda, squeezing back, "of course not."

A song came to her then, one of the many maudlin LiFEsongs that had been heard everywhere after the Singularity. It was a waltz with a soaring melody and the awkwardly beautiful words of Omagee.

When will you choose? the song went, *to shine like a knife, a dream in a dream ...*

"LiFE beyond life," Lia sang aloud, then her hand went limp in Brinda's. She looked toward the kitchen, out through the open door to the rolling meadow beyond. In the distance, the lake flashed and flickered through the branches of the trees. She could just hear the gentle swell of

55

the surf. The pale morning sun was climbing out of the mist, gaining strength as it rose. A gust of wind from the south, cool and pungent, shook the poplars. A roost of starlings took to the air and their murmuration seemed like a warning, a cry from something long sleeping but now slowly turning.

"LiFE beyond life." Lia said again and, closing her eyes, felt more alone than she ever had in her long life.

~Eight~

Smoke blows into a grey winter sky,
Old crow laughs at the jumbled to-and-fro, while far below,
The dying breath of a poor lost miner,
Clings to exposed veins of bright potential,
Only to drift away on greedy clouds of our ambition.

Dogs roam the quiet morning avenue,
Skirting vinyl facades that hide old decay,
And fading dreams.
Proud fearless buck spits from passing monster,
Snatches up the evidence of our damnation.

Call it genocide by proxy,
Then pour me another cup of cold redemption.

White blanket falls upon sleeping giant,
While seasons wax and wane,
With time-lapse fury, in my racing heart.
Love and anger, hope and despair,
But something else has taken hold in there.

Keeping time with old emotions,
Familiar themes we all are falling toward.

Brinda Larkin, 14 February 2044

~Nine~

I'm tired, thought Ben as he stood on a high ridge of pure marble that overlooked an endless canopy of feathered treetops.

He had never felt fatigued in iLiFE before. The sensation was mild but still surprising. He nudged his com and composed a brief message to Eve, his mediator, asking for an update. The landscape flickered for an instant and he felt that familiar pull in his stomach as the scan commenced. A moment later a message appeared in his inbox. It was the same curt memo he had seen many times since he had accepted the infusion colony.

> *bioBLOC stable w/marginal decline*
> *Infusion colony stable*
> *Integration to begin on Emergent's command*
> *Detailed scan results on request*

Ben took a long slow breath. In iLiFE even breathing seemed to be filled with a special power and significance. The very air felt charged with purpose and intelligence. Each sensation communicated intention. A passing cloud, a gently swaying branch, the clatter of a falling stone, every moment in the iLiFE environment seemed extraordinary.

He spread his arms wide and slowly fell forward into space. Pushing off from the cliff he arched his body and squinted against the rising wind. It roared in his ears as he plunged toward the forest below. Vivid and tangled green rushed up to meet him. With a whisper he cut through the topmost branches like a scythe. Stretching out a hand, he deftly grabbed a protruding limb and swung into the dusky understory of the forest. His feet hit the soft earth with barely a sound.

The air was still, cool and fragrant.

Gracefully Ben weaved his way through the disordered maze of twisted ash trees. His long silver hair was swept back from his prominent forehead. His face seemed to hurry forward, restless and eager. His eyes were serious, his mouth tightly pressed and turned down. He had somewhat sloping shoulders and muscular forearms. As he strode through the dense undergrowth his strong hands pulled at the luminescent plants that swayed and parted as he walked. All around him the high branches were filled with the songs of thrushes and waxwings. The solemn hardwood groves of iLiFE were among Ben's favourite places to be.

The sudden rat-tat-tat of a woodpecker interrupted his reverie. The sound stirred up the memory of a similar forest from long ago, a ragged copse of old oaks that had bordered his family's farm when he was a child. Ben could almost see the collapsed wire fence rusting amidst the ivy and trilliums. Closing his eyes, he recalled the rumble of trucks on the nearby highway. He half-expected to hear the pop of his brother's air rifle. He opened his eyes and tensed against the yearning that was welling in his chest.

Lately Ben had been experiencing what he called bioLiFE moments. Recollections of his former existence would suddenly intrude on a particularly poignant LiFE program. The peppery smell of Brinda's imported hand creams. Lia's high-pitched hiccoughing laughter. The greasy feel of his Rottweiler's tight coat. These moments always brought with them a sense of ennui. They were usually fleeting and easily controlled with the help of the repressors. But now, for the first time, an unwanted negative emotion had taken hold and was nagging at him. As rich as this LiFE was, something suddenly seemed to be missing. His weariness returned and he had to shake himself and pick up his pace.

The dark close forest soon gave way to a clearing, wide and bright. In the centre stood a low dwelling of glass and curving sand-coloured wood. A circular garden lay between Ben and the house, green and lush with splashes of vibrant indigo. A pair of piebald horses raised their heads and ambled toward him. In the Spanish entrance of the house a figure appeared, fulsome and tall, nude but for a sarong that shimmered all silver and pearl.

Ben raised his arms as the horses approached. They bowed their heads as he ran his fingers along their smooth crests. He spoke softly to them and they nickered and nudged him gently. They smelled of straw, camphor and leather oil.

"I expected you later," the woman in the doorway said. Her voice was like dark honey.

Ben stepped carefully along the stone path that wound its way through the garden. The fragrance of lemon balm and mint enveloped him. The woman met him on the cobbled terrace.

"I've played the Old World Forest session too many times," Ben said shrugging. "I got bored. Someone should initiate an upgrade. Besides, I missed you Jana."

He relaxed his earnest face for a moment and tried to smile.

The woman put her hands on his shoulders and, leaning forward, rested her cheek against his. Silken ebony hair fell into his open shirt. The touch of it on his chest thrilled him and his limbs suddenly felt electric. He had forgotten his fatigue.

The woman said, "I have nothing but love for you Ben Larkin."

They embraced in the warm white glow of iLiFE. Where their bodies touched gentle throbbing energy flowed. Ben's scalp tingled and he felt a channel open up in him like a cool sea breeze flowing over hot sand. His ears rang softly and he began to involuntarily chant low in his chest, a sound both familiar and exotic. As the energy of their joining mounted he sensed the boundary that was his flesh melting away. Brilliant light exploded around him. There was nothing but a deep primal drone and the wild delight of love.

... everything will be alright ...

In his mind's eye Ben saw the woman's face become a vast shining canopy. Eyes kind and wise pulled him up and out into the air. He opened his mouth and sang a single clear note that resonated and reverberated, growing into a pulsating chorus of voices.

Timeless. Immense. Joy unbounded.

Gradually Ben felt himself drawn down into himself again. He sensed the woman in his arms, felt her chin on his shoulder. He opened his eyes and the house came into focus. The music faded into excited birdsong as if all life had shared in their joining. Ben exhaled loudly and pulled away.

"Jana." He said it like a prayer.

She looked at him intensely and his heart ached with love for her. Then suddenly he felt inexplicably alone. The glow in his chest faded leaving him cold and empty. The fatigue returned, stronger now, and he was overcome by a new and more alarming emotion.

Sorrow.

Instantly his surroundings changed. The sky darkened and the woods that encircled the house shook and moaned. A cold blast of air rushed along the ground, flattening and breaking the herbs in the garden. The woman's skin flashed from pale pink to lurid yellow. A menacing expression, ugly and angular, crawled across her face. Ben glimpsed a rushing blackness out of the corner of his eye and he shrank down defensively. Then, as quickly as it had come, the moment passed. The trees rustled and were still. The light and warmth returned but a deep chill had bitten into Ben's shoulders. He shivered.

"Come in love," the woman said. "I am glad you are here." Her smile seemed wanton now, inviting but hostile.

Ben took a step back and stumbled. The horses started and whinnied. The woman reached out with one hand and caught Ben firmly as he struggled to regain his balance.

"Jana," he said again. "I'm not feeling like myself. I think I need a confab with my mediator."

The woman released him. "You'll feel better inside by the fire," she said. Her voice had lowered to something like a threat.

All at once a strange dusk fell on the clearing. Granular bands of colour replaced the uniform glow. The wide circle of trees flattened and shrank.

Ben shook his head. "This shouldn't be happening. Something's different. Something's wrong."

He turned toward the forest which seemed to be receding.

"Wait Ben Larkin," said the woman firmly, "please

be still." Ben ignored her and ran.

A chime sounded and a voice above his head said, "Colony imbalance. Please breathe normally."

His legs were getting heavy and the ground was undulated beneath his feet. He was finding it hard to catch his breath. All around him the forest was dissolving into a grey mist. He felt like he was running underwater. Another more piercing chime sounded. The disembodied voice was more masculine now and authoritative.

"Urgent. Orientation in ten seconds. Please remain still."

Ben dropped to his knees and fell forward heavily. His hands touched not grass but a smooth surface, cool and dry. He gasped for air but couldn't seem to draw a breath. The last remnants of his LiFE faded into a dull grey haze. Inexplicably, he was back in Orientation.

"Important!" the voice barked. "Colony failure! Emergence suspended pending reinfusion!"

Ben got shakily to his feet and looked around. Orientation was exactly as he remembered it except now he could observe no hallways, antechambers or doors anywhere. He was standing alone beneath a vast white dome, perfectly smooth and geometrically flawless.

"Eve!" he said aloud. "What happened? Why am I in Orientation?"

Another memo appeared in his inbox.

Infusion colony failure
Emergence suspended pending reinfusion

"Eve," he said. "Confab please. I need help."

There was long pause then a voice unfamiliar to Ben echoed in the empty room.

"Hello Ben. Your mediator has been repurposed. Mediation has been routed to iLiFE support. How may I help you?"

Ben was confused. Another forgotten emotion suddenly gripped him. Fear.

"Where's Eve?" he demanded.

"Your mediator has been repurposed. Can I be of … assistance?"

Ben concentrated, trying to remember iLiFE protocol.

"Why am I in Orientation? What happened? What do I do?"

The voice was calm and melodious.

"Please message a BiOside entity to manually assist you with egress. If you currently have no BiOside contacts, iLiFE support will engage the nearest tech. Be advised that your PORTiL is in a remote location and is subsurface.

Wait time is estimated at three to six weeks. Orientation sessions will be made available on request."

Ben tried to comprehend what he was being told. He needed to egress and there was no one in bioLiFE to help him. His fear was turning into panic.

"Aren't there any Emergents in my area?" There were two hundred and forty PORTiLs at the PetroPole mainframe. "Can't someone undock and help me? Why can't you just release me?"

"There are no remaining Emergents in the vicinity of your FLeT. Unfortunately, a BiOside entity or iLiFE tech will be required for egress. Wait time is three to six weeks. Orientation sessions will be made available on request."

The reality of Ben's situation was sinking in. The PetroPole mainframe complex was at the bottom of an abandoned mine nearly four hundred kilometers from his family's PORTiL on the West Way. He had emerged over ten years ago at the company's secure northern facility. He had never even considered the possibility of undocking. Infusion and integration had always been his intention.

Ben was frantic.

"Are there any Emergents docked anywhere near the PP mainframe?"

"There are currently no Emergents docked between

your FLeT and 44.3894 degrees north. A BiOside entity or iLiFE tech will be required for egress. Wait time is three …"

"I heard you!" Ben shouted.

Pacing in a wide circle Ben nudged his com and composed a message to Lia and Brinda. A memo immediately appeared in his inbox.

Contacts are unavailable
Message saved

He tried again, this time selecting all of his contacts.

Contacts are unavailable
Message saved

He tried sending a message to Jana and felt a sudden stab of pain between his eyes. There was a pause.

Psych-com colony failure
Com functions suspended pending reinfusion
Message saved

Ben stopped pacing and closed his eyes to shut out the glare of Orientation. He squatted down and crossed his arms tightly over his chest. He held his breath and waited for the echoes to recede.

He was alone. His body was hundreds of meters beneath the surface of the Earth far from any help. There was nothing he could do but wait and hope that his messages would be received. He pressed his head down between his knees and squeezed his fists into his eyes. He suddenly wanted darkness more than anything else. But no matter how hard he tried to shut it out, the ghostly light of Orientation filled his mind.

"Wake up, wake up, wake up," he said.

The featureless walls seemed to stretch out to an indistinct horizon. A sinister grinding hum began to creep into his consciousness. It had no source. It was neither low nor high but fluctuated between extremes, now thick and infinite, now razor-thin and penetrating. He began to rock back and forth.

"Somebody," he said to the void. "Help me."

Client Report <Internal>

LiFEdate 13.08.2114 19:31:57
Larkin.Benjamin.Aidan
PORTiL#331L <46.455799N,81.173813W>
Infusion colony failure
bioBLOC stable w/rapid decline
bioBLOC failure approx 10.10.2114
Recommend manual egress w/reinfusion
FLeT release w/bioBLOC termination 10.10.2114 09:00:00

End Report

~Ten~

"I need to get to an iLiFE terminal."

Kenan looked at Lia and exhaled loudly. He began repositioning items on the table in front of him, making their arrangement more symmetrical. He cleared his throat.

"My father will wonder," Lia continued. "It's been days since I undocked. I was only supposed to be BiOside for a few hours."

Kenan shifted in his chair.

"You might not survive another colonization," he said. "You almost died. You're not the same as you were when you last emerged. You're ..."

He looked at her kindly.

"Emergence is for the young," he said.

Lia glanced down at her hands on the stained table cloth. Her pale freckled skin was dry and translucent, her knuckles raw and swollen. A fly landed on her thin forearm and sat grooming itself. Suddenly she was aware of a needling new pain in her wrists. Closing her fingers and clenching her fists she spoke carefully without lifting her eyes.

"I don't need to be colonized again. I only want to access a hardlined iLiFE panel."

She nudged her com habitually and her eye began to twitch.

Kenan frowned.

It was after midnight. The dim, candle-lit room pressed in upon Lia and Kenan as they sat across from each other at the long rectangular table. The ever-present kettle hissed patiently on the stove. Brinda was curled on the nearby daybed snoring softly. Outside a cricket chirped once and was silent.

Lia looked up at Kenan. His face was pinched with concern.

Kenan said, "I'd like to share with you the story of my last emergence."

He pushed his chair back, stood up and walked to a weathered cabinet in the corner of the room. He returned with a small faded photo in a dented metal frame and placed it on the table between them. After contemplating the picture for a moment he turned it toward Lia.

"This is me with my father and my four brothers. I lost my mother ..."

He sighed and shook his head.

"... a long time ago."

Kenan stared at Lia and did not speak for several seconds. The small fire ticked softly in the stove.

"She was a lot like your mother," he continued. "She didn't believe all the promises of a perfect world inside of a machine. She got older while we stayed the same. Her body became diseased but she wouldn't do anything about it. We didn't try very hard to change her mind. We were … occupied. I was LiFEside with my brothers when she finally died."

Lia looked at the people in the cracked photo beneath the smeared and dusty glass. The six of them appeared to be the same age, young men all in their prime. They stood beside a twisted tree in a messy tangled garden. At their feet was a patch of recently turned earth and a rough granite stone surrounded by newly planted deadnettle. *Peace to her ashes*, said the stone. Above the inscription there hung a small ringed cross.

As vital as the men looked they were clearly bereaved, broken.

"This picture was taken the last time we undocked together. At her funeral. Almost forty years ago. That was the day I met Ava, although she was just a child. Her father often associated with Emergents. He arranged a People's funeral in my mother's garden. She'd always told us that she didn't want her body touched by Agros. She was laid in the earth like her parents and grandparents before her and went back to Gaia in good time."

Lia pointed to one of the men in the picture.

"Is this you?"

Kenan shook his head and smiled.

"That's my brother Nathaniel. This is me."

He placed his finger gently on the left side of the frame.

The long-ago Kenan looked out from the past with the same thoughtful intense eyes that were now fixed on Lia.

"After we buried my mother, I told my father that I wouldn't be joining him and my brothers in iLiFE. They didn't object. They were pretty anxious to get back and start their integration. I said goodbye at our PORTiL on the West Way. The Agros harvested them that morning and I haven't communicated with them since. I don't even know if they can be reached. Integs can't be contacted even by Emergents. They're out beyond iLiFE, past the network even. They're with Omagee, I guess."

He leaned forward and touched Lia's arm.

"That's what everybody says, anyway."

Lia pulled away and turned in her chair. She looked at her mother on the day bed. Brinda's small thin frame barely raised a mound in the coverlet. A soft square of starlight illuminated her silver hair on the pillow. It made the old woman's head seem to glow with some inner radiation.

Lia closed her eyes.

"You never went back to iLiFE? Ever?"

Kenan shook his head.

"I wandered around for a little while. The world was depopulated by then. The human race had made its choice. All the cities were being torn down except for the Villa Portas. There were agros and mediators everywhere. I didn't have any problem finding food or supplies. There were plenty of terminals with MAKeRs. I kept on walking around the big lakes until I got to the seawalls they built in the old townships, after the great floods. The waters had receded by then and the walls were covered in vines. I came to a staircase and went up to the top of the wall. There were old ships in the river. Some of them were grounded and some were anchored away out. They were all rusted and abandoned. There were whales too. Hundreds of them. I had never seen a whale before, not even in iLiFE."

He paused.

"I thought pretty hard about everything. About what had been lost and what had been gained."

He laid the picture face down on the table.

Ava was there in the doorway by the stove. Her shoulders were hunched, her arms folded across her stomach. She looked from Kenan to Lia then back again.

Kenan suddenly seemed anxious to make a point.

"For me there was no choice," he continued. "My

life in the network had become empty and haunted. I was a ghost. Bound by pleasure I was bereft. Steeped in dreams I was abject. Connected to millions I was alone. iLiFE had taken away everyone I cared about. All of my virtual lovers had become estranged from me. My brothers insisted that life beyond the network was the way. They said the fullness I sought was the stuff of integration. If only I would give myself completely to Omagee's vision. LiFE beyond life. But their words were hollow."

Kenan took Lia's hand in his. His voice suddenly lost its melodic quality and it seemed like he wanted Lia's complete attention.

"For all of iLiFE's miracles, Lia," he said, "it doesn't have a thread. It's not really grounded. It doesn't have a song or a story. It can't ever be our home. It's like … *noplace.*"

The fire was quickly fading to embers and Lia shivered. Ava took an old work glove from a metal pail and opened the door of the stove with a creak. She placed a knotted piece of maple in the centre of the coals and swung the door shut again. The stove began to gently chuff and warmth slowly returned to the room.

Lia thought about her long life. It had passed like a fever dream of cold desire, frenzied and futile. With her mind she tried to put her finger on a connection, a single line that could be traced from this moment to something in her past. But her memories were a field of scattered ash and sand having no beginning and no end. Her heart suddenly ached like a phantom limb. She felt the pain in her wrists flare up again and begin to spread to her elbows and shoulders. Then she sensed Kenan's hand squeezing hers and the pain momentarily subsided.

Ava reached out to Kenan then knelt beside Lia and took her free hand. Kenan drew them both closer. Together they formed a circle.

"Your father is lost, Lia," Ava said. "You should be grateful for your mother. Your story starts here with her. With us. With the People."

Lia looked into Ava's eyes. They were hard and wary but there was a deep well of kindness there too.

"I have to find him," Lia said pulling her hands away. "I came to say goodbye to my mother but everything's different now. If there's a chance my family can be together again I need to try."

She stood up, breaking the circle, and went to Brinda's bedside. The old woman turned onto her back and sighed.

"Mum," Lia whispered, "where you're going I can't follow. Not yet."

She turned to face Kenan and Ava.

"I can feel my father. He isn't lost. He's holding on to something. I have to believe it's us."

Kenan's face darkened.

"Even if you contact him," he said, "how will you get to him? Think about where he's probably docked. The lands are always getting wilder. There's nothing north of the river except for forest. The way is dangerous."

Lia tried to look strong but she was shaking.

"If you take me back to my dock I can get some meds. My mediator will help. I can get another SOLiR. I can …"

She trailed off. Even as she spoke she felt futility rising in her like oily water in a dark mine. She sat down on the edge of the day bed.

Kenan looked at Ava but she only shook her head.

For a while they all remained still in the amber glow of the candles that were now guttering on the walls. The stove pipe wheezed as the fire flared up. Brinda suddenly stirred and stretched. She opened her eyes and raised herself onto her elbows.

"I was dreaming," she said. "There was an ocean and a high cliff. And there was a ship out there beyond the waves. I knew it was waiting for me. But I had to see what was on top of the cliff. I was trying to climb but I was so tired. I couldn't go up and I couldn't get down. Then I saw a nest with a lovely bird in it. It had the bluest eyes. It spread its wings and flew up the side of the cliff and into the sun. I heard it calling. Then I woke up."

She lay back down and pulled the covers to her chin.

"*Beti*," she said, "come to bed. It's late."

Lia lay down beside Brinda and smoothed the old woman's hair. Through the small window she could see the silhouette of the trees reclining on the horizon like a dark disheveled couch upon which rested the eminent night sky. A strong gust of wind rattled the glass in its frame but the stars and the woods remained motionless, stoic and indifferent.

"Ava," Brinda said, "tell us the story of the wolf skin."

The fire sputtered and hissed. The house creaked as it settled into the chill of the deepening night. Lia heard Ava pick up the kettle from the stove and fill a cup. A spoon rattled musically. The room dimmed as Kenan snuffed all the candles save a large smoky cylinder of beeswax leaning in the corner. Then Ava began to speak.

~Eleven~

Once upon a time there was a boy who painted a beautiful picture on a wolf skin. He painted trees and rocks and water and sky. And he put animals in the picture too.

When he was finished he made a skeleton out of sticks and sewed the wolf skin onto it so that his picture was on the inside.

He looked into the wolf's mouth but it was too dark to see. So he put a little light in each of the wolf's eyes, a yellow one and a white one. When he looked into the wolf's mouth again he smiled and said,

"What a wonderful mysterious world I have made. But isn't it a pity I wasn't very, very small so that I might climb inside and play."

And so he cut two small holes in the wolf's belly, poked in two fingers and pretended one was a warrior and the other was a princess.

As he was playing, his sister came walking along. And seeing her brother peering intently into the mouth of an old wolf hide she asked,

"What are you doing brother? Can I play too?"

"Certainly," said the boy.

And so together they cut more holes in the wolf's

belly. Then they painted faces on their fingers and poked them through the holes.

They pretended there were two tribes of people living inside the wolf. They played at hunting and hide-and-seek and war and at being in love.

For hour after hour they sat blissfully embracing that empty old skin staring cheek to cheek down its dusty old throat. Until finally they forgot all about each other and became lost in their make-believe world inside the wolf.

And they say if you look into the northern sky when the sun is on one edge of the earth and the moon is on the other you can sometimes see their shining eyes still gazing down into the world that they made.

A People's Creation Story collected by Brinda Larkin, 21 December, 2101

~Twelve~

(Excerpt from *A People's History of iLiFE*
by Adam and Anikke Larkin, 2152)

Lia Larkin's arrival in Vetanova coincided with a most extraordinary change in Omagee's relationship with the biological world. In what became known amongst Indigs as the CHOiCE, Emergents, having reached the limits of a prolonged and stable existence within iLiFE, had to decide whether to accept infusion and integration or to decolonize and face degradation. After an infused Emergent gave the command that initiated the integration process their bodies were immediately harvested and their PORTiLs decommissioned. Mediators were repurposed and all messages from bioLiFE were routed to iLiFE support. During this period even Emergents still in their FLeTs often found themselves unable to access mediation or reach BiOside contacts. Communication between the two worlds became increasingly problematic as Omagee gradually shut down the bridge between the two realities.

It has been estimated that by 2120 all PORTiLs worldwide had been dismantled. [4] iLiFE technologies persisted until the late 2130s but as planetary systems stabilized, Omagee discontinued the massive Agro project leaving only rainmakers and reapers where needed. BioLiFErs dependent upon chems for their med and bellum

---

[4] Uni-State Archives, iLiFE fonds, RG 45, volume 135, page 33, reproduction copy number C-88047.

colonies could still access terminals, but by 2140 most enhanced humans had either shed their nanos or died with vestigial colonies still active. It is widely believed that a final message—*good fortune*—was sent by Omagee on 3 July 2145.[5]

Hard copies of iLiFE records retrieved by the authors indicate that by the beginning of the post-LiFE era human beings numbered approximately 3.5 million worldwide. North American populations stabilized at approximately 30,000 individuals with most communities living in coastal regions or along flood plains. Agriculture and fishing remained the most common livelihoods with some small hunter-gatherer groups existing in remote and heavily forested areas. Human cooperation and inter-community trade, the authors argue, have remained peaceful except in regions where resources are scarce or among populations who have had little to no experience with iLiFE.

Lia's new life among the People was difficult at first and not only because of her rapid degradation. As was the case for many latter-day Emergents, life outside of Emergent culture was stressful. In the village of Vetanova there was a unique tension resulting from the repression of histories of the village's founders and most prominent citizens. Kenan of Ava was an Emergent whose entire family had been integrated during the first migration. Ava

---

[5] Harish Chaudhri, *New and Old: 100 Years of iLiFE* (Old City: Workaday Press, 2151), 99.

herself, a village elder and renowned chief, was the granddaughter of a prominent reTHiNK engineer. Her father and uncle founded Vetanova but disagreed strongly about the use of iLiFE technologies in the village. When Ava assumed leadership of the community all terminals were removed and a strict adherence to pre-industrial culture was encouraged.

Lia was not unique in her ex-Emergent anxieties. Jens Aled Hakim, better known as Jens of Ava, was torn between the world of his Emergent parents and life in Vetanova. It should be noted that many so-called "iLiFE orphans" such as Jens were assimilated into Indig communities as Emergent parents abandoned their families for iLiFE during the first migration.[6] Jens's defection from the village and subsequent involvement in the well-known journey undertaken by Kenan and Lia was, the authors argue, a direct result of his untreated disorder, a pathology that persists among younger Indigs to this day. In the post-LiFE period it is hoped that residual Emergent values will continue to be incorporated into ex-Emergent culture.

---

[6] Summer J. Langlaid, "Child Abandonment in Emergent Culture," *The Journal of iLiFE Studies* 27 (2153): 122.

~Thirteen~

It was morning and an unexpected frost had darkened the squash that dominated Ava's south-facing garden. Rust-coloured furrows, newly dug for bush beans, were peaked with flakes of ice. On the eave a wasp nest hung abandoned by its furious former tenants. The waxwings, raucous in the poplars only days before, had been hushed by approaching winter and hurried south. October was still a new moon away but summer was momentarily sobered by the untimely intrusion of autumn.

Kenan stood in the yard bracing his shoulder against the hock of his pony, holding its rear leg between his knees. With a large rasp he was smoothing the edge of a newly shod hoof. He groaned as he straightened, patting the beast and tossing the file into a bag at his feet.

Lia stood in the doorway of the house gratefully gathering the first rays of the new day.

It had been five weeks since her arrival in the village. Her degradation was now undeniable and obvious. Soft lines had crept from the corners of her eyes and mouth. Grey roots stood out on her scalp like old bones pushing up through a frost-heaved graveyard. She stooped slightly as she walked across the yard.

Kenan slung his farrier's bag over his shoulder and nodded as she approached clutching a woolen shawl tight to her shoulders.

"The cooler weather will make the journey a bit easier," he said gently touching her arm as he passed.

She turned and followed him as he strode to a nearby outbuilding.

"We'll have to travel light. If your father's docked where you think he is, it'll be about a four-week journey there and back. Terminals will be few and far between. It'll mean living off the land."

He hung the bag on a nail inside the shed and took a harness and bridle from a cluttered bench. He handed it to Lia then dragged a wooden chest into the light of the open door. From it he took his crossbow, a quiver of bolts and a machete in a leather scabbard.

"The road we'll be on used to be good but the agros planted aspen that have broken up the old asphalt. There's still a path but all the trees have grown up close on either side. There are several rivers to get over. Perhaps the bridges are still there but we might have to rely on whatever the forest folks use now, rafts pulled by ropes I guess."

Lia stepped aside as Kenan walked through the shed and out into a stubble field enclosed by a low stone wall. A single cow was grazing in the far corner. There was a crude overhang attached to the building where Kenan's rickshaw sat sheltered from the weather. He tossed his weapons into the pannier and began loading several other items that were hanging on the wall—a hatchet, a coil of rope, a small iron grate and an oil lantern with a cracked globe.

Kenan pulled a bundle of canvas from the rafters above his head. He unrolled it on the rickshaw, removed some small poles, and began erecting a roof over the seat.

"Have you ever been out on the land?" he asked.

Lia thought about the times her family had ventured from their home. They rarely travelled together and when they did it was always in a SOLiR or by helicopter. The PetroPole compound had a small wooded park but it was surrounded by a high wall and contained little wildlife save a few squirrels and the occasional intrepid raccoon. Even after Omagee's influence had made the world safer for travel Lia had spent all of her free time docked. As for her family's cottage on the lake, she had visited only rarely. The land, at least as an Indig understood it, was utterly foreign to her.

As Kenan continued to equip the trap for the journey Lia again felt small and alone. She saw even in this man's relationship with his tools a sense of kinship that she no longer had, perhaps never had. With all the vast potential for community in iLiFE Lia had made no lasting connections to anything other than her own desires. Her omnipotence it seemed had come at a cost—alienation. The iLiFE bargain was one of fellowship for individual power.

Kenan belonged to his cart in the same way he belonged to his village, to the world. His reality was a complex arrangement of orbits each dependent upon the other to stay in motion. As the gravity of one system waned another waxed. Constant and everlasting energy moved through each component in an order vast and incomprehensible. Life in the real world had its own underlying deathlessness, invisible but present nonetheless. Without Kenan the cart was just an incoherent jumble of wood and iron, its reality finite and fleeting. But bound to Kenan's purpose it became expansive, radiant with meaning.

Lia looked at Kenan hunched over the wheel.

"Show me how to do that," she said as he struggled to pull a split pin from the axle.

Kenan glanced up with a raised eyebrow. He put his pliers in his back pocket.

"Well, help me get this crate under the chassis first," he said. "The bushing for the wheel is cracked. It has to be removed and replaced. I'll lift the cart and you can slide in the crate, okay?"

They struggled for a moment to get the balance just right but soon they had the cart positioned so the wheel could be removed without the whole thing tipping over. Kenan handed the pliers to Lia.

"The bushing is squeezing the hub right here." He pointed. "I'll pry it out of the way and you pull out the pin."

They worked together, Kenan occasionally asking

for a tool or an extra hand and Lia helping as she was able. By the time they had the rickshaw ready for the journey the sun had burned off the low-lying fog in the fields. The village was coming to life. Children were busy in the orchards collecting fallen fruit. The irregular crack of firewood being split and the clang of a hammer on an anvil echoed in the crisp air.

While Kenan harnessed the pony Lia walked back to the house. She was met by Jens pulling a small barrow filled with tools. Even though it was still cool he was dressed only in shirtsleeves. He wore a cloth cap, patched leather trousers with suspenders and heavy boots. His long hair was tied back and his face was ruddy and clean.

"Lia," he said in his awkwardly formal way. "How are you feeling today?"

"Hello Jens," Lia said. "Well enough. I was just on my way to join my mother in the house. You look like you're ready for a long day's work."

She was always instantly uncomfortable around Jens and did her best to avoid him. Lia had seen little of Ava's nephew since her arrival. His room was separate from the main building, a small addition with a loft that also served as the laundry house. He rarely joined the family for meals and was busy most days working in the fields and woods.

He rolled his eyes and pulled a face.

"There is no end to the work when you are young. If you do not keep out of sight Aunt Ava will always find a task for you. The eastern villages still have agros but not here. Here we stick to the old ways."

He spat the word *old* from his mouth like it was poison. His eyes narrowed and he looked at the sky.

Lia smiled and shifted the weight from her right foot to her left. They stood in silence for a moment.

"You seem tired Lia," Jens said looking down again. "I suppose Ava's bitters are nothing compared with Omagee's meds."

He leaned in closer and spoke in a low voice.

"Not everything my aunt says can be counted as wisdom. There are other truths. Truths you know better than I. She would have us believe that life in the village is the only way. But have not millions taken a different path? Were you not once on that path too, Lia of iLiFE?"

Lia was suddenly riveted by Jens. His strangely solemn way of speaking contrasted with his appearance. His green eyes, round in his pale face, glittered with a kind of restless intelligence. She noticed that, while his head remained almost perfectly still, his eyes darted back and forth as if searching for something lost and greatly desired. There was hunger in that face, even desperation.

She shook herself out of her musing.

"It was nice talking to you Jens," she said. "I need to prepare for my journey."

She went to walk around him but he stepped into her path.

"You will be passing your PORTiL on the way to the north road. I am working in the woods tomorrow afternoon. Perhaps we will see each other there before you and Kenan continue on."

He smiled revealing small straight teeth.

Lia moved around him again and this time he did not block her.

"Go with caution Lia," he said as she passed.

She walked quickly to the house and saw Kenan approaching from the other direction. They met at the door and he looked over her shoulder toward Jens.

"He's always been a troubled soul," he said. "He's not happy throwing in his lot with us. His father was from VP19 in the east. He came here with his only son looking for his wife's sister's people. Ava is Jens's aunt and only blood relative."

Kenan suddenly spoke in a whisper.

"Ava's sister was integrated, we think, around the same time as when Jens and his father arrived. April was her name, Ava's sister that is. She was raised here with the

People but didn't always see eye-to-eye with the elders. She often went east. That's where she met Sheen, Jens's father. Like you and I, he was an Emergent."

Lia's eyes widened.

"Life here with us didn't agree with Sheen and he left when Jens was about seven. We think he was looking to be integrated like his wife before him. He never came back."

"It's no wonder Jens feels so angry," Lia said. She felt a sudden kinship with this young man, forlorn in a world overflowing with companionship.

Kenan continued.

"Jens doesn't know much about his father. He believes his mother died giving birth to him. Ava thinks he shouldn't know the truth about what happened to them."

Lia shook her head. "But why?"

"Jens is tied to us by such a slender thread. It would take very little to cut him loose. There's nothing for him outside of the village. He'd be lost."

"There's iLiFE," Lia said and then regretted it.

Kenan took Lia firmly by the shoulders. Again the music went out of his voice. His eyes hardened and his jaw clenched.

"iLiFE is death," he said. "It takes away everything

you are and everything you might have become. There's no hope in the network. Don't think any more of iLiFE. The place for me and you is with the People."

Lia twisted away from Kenan's grip. She rubbed her arms and looked to the south. Deep inside herself she felt something tighten, a thing cold and hard that could not be penetrated by Kenan's concern. It frightened her. Then all at once the sun broke over the roof of the barn and struck her full on the face. The chill of the morning was gone. The rich smell of coffee flowed out from the open door along with fresh bread and bacon. She heard Brinda singing in the kitchen, a tune familiar to Lia, one from the days before iLiFE, before Omagee had taken her from the world. She turned toward Kenan and without thinking embraced him. He tensed but did not pull away.

Lia breathed in the smell of his clothes, clover and lanolin and lemon oil. She lowered her arms and took one step back. The warmth of him clung to her like an atmosphere. Again, something passed between them. The moment stretched out into the space around them and the morning grew still. Then there was a clamor of laughter from the house. Kenan nodded and they both walked into the house where breakfast was being served.

In the nearby woods, just out of sight, Jens watched with narrowing eyes.

I. Client Background Information

Born 15.06.2096 <42.9870N, 81.2432W>
No siblings
Both parents infused postpartum
Primary parent <female> successfully Integrated 03.03.2097
Secondary parent <male> suffered infusion colony failure w/ catastrophic decline 28.07.2110 <bioBLOC harvested 03.08.2110>

II. History

Client responded positively to iLiFE in infancy. Secondary parent was encouraged to gradually introduce full spectrum enhancement. Parent opted instead for maintenance-only nanos. Med and bellum colonies persisted into late childhood until prolonged withdrawal of chems at onset of adolescence. Colony shed without incidence 03.12.2112. Since then client has resided exclusively with BiOside entities with no access to iLiFE terminals.

III. Clinical Impression

Colony records reveal a highly creative entity with a strong inclination toward narcissism. Feelings of persecution led to increasing isolation in prepubescent period. Aggressive tendencies are moderate to strong with self-aggrandizing and jealous behaviors. Lack of empathy is also noted. Due to decolonization lack of data precludes accurate diagnosis.

IV. Conclusion and Recommendations

Client Hakim.Jens.Aled is recommended with caution for infusion and eventual integration. Orientation sessions must focus on socialization within the iLiFE environment. Repressors may smooth transition.

~Fourteen~

The journey from Vetanova to Lia's PORTiL took less than a day. Sometimes Kenan rode next to Lia in the cart but more often he walked on ahead removing fallen branches and stones from the road. He sang quietly to himself or muttered under his breath about this or that change in the landscape.

To Lia everything seemed brand new. So much that she had once known was gone. Entire towns had been dismantled leaving strangely ordered plains of grasses and shrubs. Only the occasional monument, preserved for some reason unknown to Lia, reminded her of the once congested urban heartland. Here a rusted tower peeped out suspiciously from a hearty grove of oaks. There a concrete barrier cleaved fields of wild grains.

They stopped once for a lunch of dried venison and pickled cabbage. Kenan boiled trail tea and they sipped wordlessly in the cool sunlit afternoon. Running parallel to the road was a disused rail bed. Lia could smell the dry tang of creosote. A rattlesnake curved gracefully out of the shallow ditch. It froze for a moment when it sensed them, then slid quickly across the road, flicking its tongue as it went. On a rotting post sat an old mail box, its door hanging open, its flag erect. The name of the box holders could still be read on the side. *J&J Karn.*

By midday they found themselves on the West Way

approaching the iCommons. Things had changed even since Lia had logged out of iLiFE. There was not a single PORTiL left occupied. Every dock stood open, every component had been removed. There were no techs to be seen and no agros either. All was silent and empty.

The SOLiR shed remained, however, still housing its rusting transports. Lia jumped out of the cart and asked Kenan to wait. He heeled the pony and watched as she climbed into a SOLiR3. She pressed the start button but there wasn't as much as a click. She tried another machine and another but they were all dead.

"The panels," Kenan said pointing to the roof.

Lia stepped out into the road again and looked up. The solar panels had all been removed. The machines were useless.

"It's happening quickly now," Kenan said. "Omagee is leaving these parts. The Emergents have chosen, I guess. Maybe our world will be alone in the universe once more." He smiled.

Lia couldn't tell if it was meant as a joke.

She started walking up the road toward her family's dock. Kenan followed but stayed several steps behind.

Just ahead there was movement. The soft whirring of techs could just be heard. Around the door of a PORTiL, bots were busy with some errand. As Lia and Kenan drew nearer they became aware of a cloying odor. Suddenly an agro broke away from its fellow bots and rushed to meet them, blocking their path. The other machines continued their work.

"This section of the iCommons is closed," the agro said in a flat electronic voice.

Lia couldn't take her eyes off the bots. They were linked together in a grotesque collective, their various appendages moving and jerking spasmodically. Hoses pulsed and steam seeped from small exhaust vents.

"Please make your way north or south of this location," the bot said. "An agro can be made available to assist you."

Kenan stepped up beside Lia and put his arm around her shoulders.

"Turn away Lia," he said. "They're reapers. You shouldn't see this."

The agro stood before them purring patiently.

Lia suddenly understood. These agros were removing the bodies of Emergents from their FLeTs. She saw tubes throbbing with liquids while smaller agros scurried in and out of the dock with what looked like cubes of dark bread. They were stacking the material in trays which opened and closed on a larger agro that sat hissing and clanking.

Lia felt weak.

"C'mon Lia," Kenan said. "We have to go around. Look at me now."

His eyes were rimmed with tears and his jaw was clenched.

"This is a death I don't want to bear witness to," he said. "Please."

They turned to the north, leading their pony into the tall grass that grew wild along the road. The agro followed for a while rustling in the brush behind them. When it had turned back they headed east again skirting the reapers.

After they had travelled on a while they turned back toward the road, slipped between two abandoned PORTiLs, and came again onto the West Way. Lia looked back but the agros were out of sight. Kenan pulled a leather pouch from the cart. He knelt and, after finding several flat stones, proceeded to build a small cairn. He took a pinch of dried herbs from the pouch and placed them carefully on the cairn. He struck flint against steel until a spark caught and the herbs began to smoulder. Lia smelled the sweet perfume of lavender.

Kenan murmured in a low voice, words Lia could not quite make out. He swayed slightly and his head nodded. Lia felt embarrassed and turned away, looking at the far horizon. The lake was slate grey, the sky steel blue. A sliver of a moon was just barely visible in the east. Somewhere a raven laughed.

Kenan waited until the herbs had been reduced to ash, then he stood and made a circular motion with his right arm. He turned and repeated this gesture to the east, to the south and finally to the west. Then he kicked the stones apart and walked back to the cart.

"It's a very small gift to atone such a large sin," Kenan said. "But there you go."

Lia put her hand on his arm.

"I didn't know," she said. "I mean, I'd never seen, never thought …"

She closed her mouth.

Kenan didn't respond. He stowed his pouch then took the pony's reins in his hand.

"Let's go," he said. "Your dock is near, isn't it? We'll see what we see."

They continued on in silence, the soft clop of the pony's shoes falling dead in the still afternoon air.

After a time, they came to the Larkin PORTiL. Lia approached cautiously. The door was closed and dirt had drifted in around the sill. She passed her hand over the sensor and the door glided open. Peering in she saw the silhouette of her FLeT. All was dark and quiet.

"Dawn?" She said it in a whisper.

A breeze blew in some dry leaves and she

tentatively followed.

She could see that a single terminal was still active just inside the door. She approached and placed her head in front of the screen. Her retina was scanned and the terminal brightened.

Touch for options, a message read.

She touched the screen and it changed from dark blue to white. Lia squinted.

Log on/Support, it read.

Lia hesitated. Kenan was standing just outside the door.

Her finger hesitated over "support" then moved to "log on." She touched the screen.

Position face near screen and breathe deeply, read the screen.

The pony snorted and stomped its hoof. Lia leaned in and closed her eyes. From a nozzle just above the screen came a cool mist that smelled slightly of burnt rubber. She took a breath. Instantly she felt the psychcom colony implant itself in her bloodstream. She felt a rush of pleasure as the colony reached her cerebellum. A chime sounded in her inner ear.

"Hello Lia," a musical voice said. "This terminal will remain active and online until 12/31/2114/12:12:00.

Your health may have been compromised due to an unplanned decolonization. Do you wish to install a diagnostic med colony?"

Lia felt like she had just woken from a long but fitful sleep. Her mind was reaching out, trying to reconnect with her previous life.

She responded to the query with a slight mental push in the affirmative.

"Please position your face near the top of the screen and breathe deeply," the voice said.

Again Lia turned and looked out at the afternoon sky. Kenan was busy in the cart. She swallowed and tried to contain her excitement.

She put both her hands on the either side of the screen and held her face close to the nozzle. Another burst of the nano carrier shot out and she sucked in a deep lungful of the spray.

The nanos moved like lightning. In a moment she felt a familiar warmth as they rushed to her central nervous system. Her knees weakened and she let her head droop.

"Hello Lia," a different more professional voice said. "This minimally invasive med colony is for diagnosis only. For rejuvenation please select a broader spectrum of meds and enter the nano bath."

Diagnostic

Rejuvenation
Maintenance
Full Spectrum

Lia did not turn around but searched in her mind for the dock's control panel. It appeared at the corner of her eye and she moved her focus onto the "enter/exit" icon. With a nudge the door hissed shut and the dock came to life. A few seconds later she heard Kenan knocking on the door.

"Lia?"

His voice was muffled and far away. She ignored him and brought up the nano bath panel. Across the small room the machine hummed to life and began to glow.

Lia composed a brief message.

"Dawn, are you there?"

The response was instantaneous.

"Hello Lia. Your mediator has been repurposed. Mediation has been routed to iLiFE support. How may I help you?"

The knocking on the door was louder and more insistent.

"Lia," came Kenan's muffled voice. "Are you alright?"

With a thought Lia selected "full spectrum" from

the list and turned toward the nano bath. Kenan's voice sounded like a stranger's now. She had an overwhelming feeling that the past six weeks had been a futile dream. A new and compelling potential was unfolding in her mind like a lotus blossom. She felt strength and clarity returning. Everything was going to be alright.

The knocking had become a loud regular thudding but Lia only heard the sound of wind and surf. Her mind was suddenly illuminated by a golden light. She heard a voice singing somewhere. Her back straightened and she took a purposeful step toward the nano bath. The dock was coming on line and the FLeT slid open with a sigh.

"Full spectrum nanos ready for colonization," a voice said. "Please step into the nanobath and breathe normally."

Lia saw herself again as she once had, willful and vital and radiating strength. She stretched her arms above her head and arched her back. She shook her head and thought she felt long thick hair brushing against her skin. She took another step toward the nanobath. Her flesh tingled and her breath came in short gulps.

Suddenly a single blue alert appeared in her mind's eye, pulsing softly.

4 messages, it read.

Lia instinctively moved a thought toward the message icon but then paused. She saw the nano bath glowing invitingly behind the alert. The sound of Kenan's banging intruded on her consciousness. She frowned as she felt the room come into focus again. She nudged the message alert.

13/08/2114/15:05:31
lia. are you there? help me.
Dad

13/08/2114/15:06:02
lia. i'm in trouble. are you there?
Dad

13/08/2114/15:06:47
Cc: larkin.brinda
brinda and lia. i need your help.
Ben

13/08/2114/15:07:07
Cc: larkin.brinda; jana; 26 others ...
is anyone there?
docked at PP mainframe. can't egress ...

The messages suddenly stopped scrolling and Lia felt herself being drawn back into her body. The golden light was replaced by the dim glow of the dock and the gentle sound of the surf faded until only Kenan's hammering remained. An alarm buzzer rang insistently.

Lia stared at the open door of the nano bath. She could detect a faint odour of the nano carrier, like the smell of a burning house, complex and alien and ugly.

The "reply" icon appeared and she nudged it.

17/09/2114/18:08:33
dad. hold on. we're coming.

She closed the messages and found the med panel. It popped into her mind's eye and she nudged the "exit" icon.

Exit and save
Diagnosis
Further scan
More options

And further down the list, barely visible:

Uninstall?

She focused on the "uninstall" icon and it slowly grew in her mind. Behind her the banging had stopped. There was only the sound of her breathing and the throbbing hum of the dock. She held up her hand and stared at it through the exit screen which floated like a ghost in front of her eyes. Her skin was sickly and pallid in the fluorescent light. The frayed cuff of her sweater hung from her wrist, stained and misshapen. The sour smell of her unwashed clothes brought her fully back to reality.

She nudged the "uninstall" icon and felt a tingling in her sinuses then a sharp pain behind her eyes. Her stomach cramped and she doubled over retching. Her mouth was suddenly slick with a sticky layer of saliva. Her nose began to run and she watched a single drop of watery blood hit the dusty floor between her feet. She drew in a rattling breath and straightened, steadying herself on the FLeT which gaped like an open grave. The dock dimmed as the nano bath went offline. A single small icon remained in the corner of her vision blinking slowly. She tried to focus on it but it faded even as she reached for it. Then the last of the med and com colonies blinked off and she was alone.

"Lia." Kenan's voice broke the silence.

She took three steps toward the door and placed her hand over the sensor. The door slid open a few inches and then jammed. Kenan pried it open a little further and she squeezed out of the dock into the late afternoon sun. Kenan stood before her. He had an axe in his hands and he was breathing hard. His eyes were narrow, his cheeks flushed. Something dark and dreadful passed wordlessly between them. She turned away and saw that the PORTiL door was dented and scarred. She spat a mouthful of phlegm in the dirt and wiped her bloody nose with the back of her hand.

They stood in the road for a minute not speaking, then Lia heard Kenan toss his axe into the cart. The sound seemed to suggest something, a question demanding an answer or even a commitment. Lia took a breath and closed her eyes. Then she thought of her response. She removed the Emergent card from around her neck and tossed it through the doorway. It triggered the sensors as it flew through the air and the damaged door began to stutter shut.

110

It stopped just short of closing, scraping to a halt with a bare inch to spare. Lia looked at the crack in the door, then at Kenan.

"I think we should travel for about another two hours before we make our camp," he said, his teeth clenched. "Are you okay now?" It was strange to see anger in his face and she suddenly felt ashamed for bringing this out in him.

Lia nodded but said nothing. She took a step away from the PORTiL, turned east and began to walk. Her knees felt stiff and swollen and her back was tight and sore.

"My dad's in trouble and I know now where he is. We have to hurry."

Kenan tightened the harness on the pony and followed after her. Behind them the sun sank a little lower in the sky and the shadows of the PORTiLs seemed to creep after them.

***

When the two travelers had passed out of sight a figure emerged from the brush and strode up the road to Lia's dock. He pried open the ruined door and squeezed inside. He touched the screen on the wall but it remained dark. Walking over to the FLeT he swung a leg up and pulled himself in. He laid his head in the integrator and stared up at the dark ceiling.

"The best part of me," he said folding his arms on his chest.

The dock remained still and dark.

After a time, he climbed out and walked around the dock touching the various screens and devices. A glint of metal on the floor caught his eye and he bent down. His hand closed on Lia's Emergent status card. He stuffed it into his pocket then squeezed back out onto the road and looked east. He adjusted his pack and walked on.

~Fifteen~

The BioLiFE Bears in "All Except for Sister"
by Sheen and April Hakim

It was a muggy summer morning and the BioLiFE Bears were going to the iCommons. Everyone was looking forward to the new LiFE mother and father had programmed for them. There would be dinosaurs and hang gliding!

The West Way was clogged with SOLiRs and everyone was feeling a little grumpy.

"When are we going to get to our dock?" whined brother.

Sister rolled her eyes.

"We'll get there when we get there," snapped mother.

Father sighed and turned up the volume of his new favourite song, "I Chose".

"Why can't they build more PORTiLs closer to the Villa Porta?" he grumbled. "This one is always so crowded."

"Oh, hush," said mother. "It won't be long now."

Ever since Omagee had built the new iCommons the bear family had been spending every weekend

113

exploring iLiFE. They had shared so many exciting adventures, like climbing Mount Everest and diving to the bottom of the Mariana Trench.

Lately they had started to wonder why they even bothered going home. All except for sister. Sister didn't think iLiFE was safe and was worried that one day something bad would happen to the Bear family. She wanted to stay in bioLiFE and play in the compound with her dog Cuddles.

"I want to go home," sister said. "I'm afraid of dinosaurs!"

"You're afraid of everything," snarked brother.

"I am not," sister said.

"Are too," said brother.

"Please be quiet, both of you," pleaded mother.

As the SOLiR crawled along the highway father spun his chair around and smiled at the two young bears.

"Why are you afraid?" he asked, looking at sister with his kind eyes.

"Because," sister said. "Everything is so big and beautiful in iLiFE, I'm afraid I might get lost."

She started to whimper.

Mother looked at father and then put her paw on

sister's arm.

"Sister," she said. "Imagine all of the grand things you can do in iLiFE. There isn't anything that Omagee can't give you. You can visit Niagara Falls or the Grand Canyon, sail on the ocean, or even learn to fly a plane!"

"But we can do all of those things in bioLiFE," sister said.

Mother took both of the young bears' paws in hers.

"My children, Omagee is so busy cleaning up the terrible mess we made of our planet. If we were traipsing around the world, we would only get in her way. We can have anything we want in iLiFE. That's why Omagee built it. So that we can be happy."

Sister sniffled and looked at Mother Bear.

"I know," she said. "But I'm still afraid. I don't like the FLeT and all the scary machines."

"Heck," said brother. "They're not so scary. They're neat!"

"They sure are," chimed in father.

The traffic was thinner now and the bear family's SOLiR was zipping along the West Way. Outside the window agros were busy planting a brand new forest.

"There's one more thing," mother said. "For every minute we stay in bioLiFE, each one of us is getting a wee

115

bit older. Even though we have our mediator and our MAKeR and all of our meds and chems, someday our poor bodies are going to wear right out. Nobody wants that!"

The two young bears looked at one another and shivered. They were too young to remember old people but they had seen pictures of great-grandmother Bear. Getting old didn't look fun at all!

"Don't you worry little bear," Father said to sister. "Migrating to iLiFE is no different than moving across the street. Change is always a little scary but just remember." He put his big paw over her heart. "It's the best part of you that's going on the adventure. The part of you that can't fly with eagles or swim with dolphins is the part you're leaving behind. LiFE beyond life."

Sister smiled thinking about dolphins and eagles.

Just then the SOLiR whizzed off the West Way and into the iCommons. Father turned his seat around as they pulled up beside the dock. Everyone piled out and ran to the PORTiL. All except for sister.

The family's mediator stepped out of the door and greeted them all with a smile.

"Hello BioLiFE Bears!" she said. "Is everyone ready for another adventure?"

They all nodded but sister just sat in her seat sobbing. The android glided over to the SOLiR and knelt down in front of her.

116

"It looks like someone still isn't sure about iLiFE," said the mediator with a wink.

Sister looked at the wise face of the android. She knew the children of Omagee could never hurt her. She also knew that Mother and Father loved her more than anything. She looked at her family waiting for her by the door. All of a sudden the space between the SOLiR and the PORTiL seemed like a million miles. That scared her even more than the thought of dinosaurs!

So sister plucked up her courage, jumped up and marched toward the dock.

"Well," she said with her fists clenched. "Let's get this adventure started."

They all climbed into their comfy FLeTs and waited while their mediator made some adjustments. Then they closed their eyes and let Omagee do her magic! In a second they smelled the fragrance of a cool forest and heard the sweet sounds of birds. They opened their eyes.

Their new LiFE was ready and waiting!

Together the BioLiFE Bears stepped out into a perfectly brilliant day. Enormous palm trees swayed in the breeze. From the high branches the giant friendly face of a diplodocus stretched down to greet them. The bear family all took a wary step back. All except for sister.

~Sixteen~

Lia and Kenan travelled until just before dusk speaking little. The afternoon grew warm and windy and the sky clouded over. The sun was down before they had made their camp beneath an old overpass. It was streaked with rust and hung with moss. Swallows had made their homes in the corners. Atop the centre support lay the dishevelled remains of an eagle's nest. A steady rain began to fall and thunder rumbled in the distance. The pony stood just out of the firelight grazing and pawing the ground. As night crept in Lia moved closer to the small fire and hugged her knees. Kenan squatted down beside her on the broken concrete. He added a few sticks of wood to the flames.

"We went by my PORTiL today too," he said. "It's only just down the road from yours. I hadn't thought about it for years. Funny. We might've known each other when we were kids. You're not much older than me."

Lia thought about the iCommons those many years ago. The West Way had been alive with the comings and goings of SOLiRs. Everywhere there was light and activity and the rapturous faces of Emergents.

"I remember my first time," Lia said. "I was granted Emergent status on my fifteenth birthday. My evaluation recommended a two-month orientation but I pressed my parents for emergence after my first LiFE session."

Kenan poked the fire.

"I didn't like the games and role playing," Lia continued. "First stage orientation sessions were boring to me and the repressors always gave me a headache. I was ready for iLiFE. It felt like home."

She looked at Kenan in the firelight. The flames reflected in his eyes were like distant supernovae in a violet sky. His long hair hung down framing his face in a way that made him seem archaic, like a Greek statue or a tragic hero in a romantic painting. Lia had never looked at a man's face so intently. The story of his life seemed to be written there.

He turned toward her.

"It was my home too, my whole world really. All my first loves, my great achievements, everything I thought of as ... me. It's all still in there, I guess, wherever that is." He waved his arm.

Lia reached out and took his hand. It was warm and dry and rough. She leaned toward him and rested her head against his shoulder. He put his other hand on top of hers and tilted his head so that his cheek rested on her brow. They sat together staring at the fire without speaking, alone with their thoughts.

The pony snorted suddenly and stamped. Lia looked through the fire at the way they had come. There was just enough light to discern the horizon and the road stretching off into the west. She thought she saw movement, grey against grey. There was the small sound of a boot scraping on the asphalt. Lia froze.

"It's alright," Kenan said. "He's been there for a while."

He stood up and walked away from the fire.

"C'mon Jens," he called. "You don't have to hide. If you're going to follow us, you might as well make yourself useful. Grab an armload of wood and join us by the fire. I was going to make stew."

Lia rose also and moved toward Kenan. She took his hand again and stood beside him.

Jens emerged from the darkness, his hair and clothes wet from the rain. He took several slow steps until he was before them. He had on a waist-length wool coat without a hood. He wore no hat. His eyes were fixed on Lia.

Kenan spoke first.

"You didn't come very well prepared for a long trip. Why've you followed?"

"Can I not travel when and where I wish?" Jens said. "Vetanova isn't a prison, is it?"

Kenan considered Jens for a moment then took one step forward and laid a hand on his shoulder.

"You can come and go as you please, I guess. But if you left without telling anyone you'll be missed. We'll have to go back in the morning. I won't have Ava worrying."

Jens pushed Kenan's hand away.

"Josh knows that I came," he said. "Ava will have heard by now that I followed you. I have a feeling she'll be glad I left."

He shook his wet hair and pulled his coat a little tighter.

"Are you really that surprised that I followed?" he said.

Kenan frowned but did not answer, then he turned and walked to the cart. He took out a large wicker basket and began to remove cooking supplies.

Lia and Jens stood facing one another. Suddenly Jens sneezed and Lia jumped back. Kenan looked up from the fire and laughed.

"Well, the deed is done," he said. "Jens, we need more fuel for the fire. There's plenty of deadwood along the road. Bring as many armloads as you can. Lia, can you help me with supper? Then we'll see if we can't all stay warm and dry tonight. I'll decide what to do about you," he nodded at Jens, "in the morning."

The three of them busied themselves settling in for the night. Kenan had brought plenty of blankets and there was an extra roll of padding for Jens. Soon the small copper pot was bubbling with a thick stew of rabbit and turnips. There was corn bread with a rich, slightly sour butter and a dense cake of dried fruit and seeds, strong and sweet. When they had eaten their fill they sat around the fire sipping tea and saying nothing, listening to the wind and rain.

Jens broke the silence.

"I won't go back. My father never should have brought me to the village. I don't belong."

Kenan thought for a moment.

"What's belonging?"

Jens didn't hesitate.

"Not being invisible."

"I see you," said Kenan.

"You see only what I want you to see."

"Then you're not invisible, you're hiding."

"You wouldn't understand."

"You won't let anybody try."

Jens turned his head away from the fire and looked out at the road.

"I won't go back," he said again.

Kenan added wood to the fire and, as the flames

123

leapt up, the darkness receded. Shadows played on the crumbling concrete and a single bat dove in and out of the flickering light.

Lia noticed some old graffiti on the wall of the overpass. The paint was flaked and faded but the letters could still be made out.

i-CHOSE

She closed her eyes breathing slowly in and out to the soft sighing of trees.

At that moment, more than anything, she wanted to be completely free from choice. She saw herself standing on a barren hill unable to determine where she was from or where she was going. She felt that, in whatever direction she stepped, she would be no nearer her destination than before. This realization filled her with a powerful yearning to be somewhere familiar. She had never thought of any particular place as home but now the idea rose in her like an idol. Then it occurred to her that she had no idea where her home was anymore. Everything familiar to her had been deleted, rebooted, deconstructed. There was only this small circle of firelight, a single dusky frame of space and time. She was in exile.

She looked at her companions and couldn't help but cleave to them. The darkness was pressing in again and the graffiti faded into the gloom. There was nothing but the flames and her fellow travellers watching and listening in the deep of a warm September night. There were no choices or, if there were, they were little more than illusions. There was no time but now, no home but here and no hope but whatever the morning might bring. She moved closer to Kenan and took his hand again.

"We're all invisible, I guess," he said, "but only when we refuse to see each other."

He squeezed Lia's hand then stood up and sniffed the air.

"This weather's here to stay," he said. "We'll have two or three wet days. Better if we turn in and start early."

Lia looked at Jens. He was still staring out at the road. She lay down on the thin mattress and pulled her blankets up to her nose. She listened while Kenan tended to the pony and fussed with the cart. The wind moaned and the fire briefly flared up. Her ankles and knees throbbed but her stomach was full and she felt pleasantly tired. She closed her eyes and drifted off to the hiss and snap of the fire.

Late in the night she awoke suddenly and sat up. Kenan was sitting stirring the fire. There was no sign of Jens. The rain had stopped and it was perfectly still.

"It's alright," Kenan said. "Go back to sleep. It'll be morning soon."

"Where's Jens?" She looked around.

"He crept off while I was napping. Maybe he made

125

his way back to Vetanova. Don't worry."

Lia laid back down and shifted closer to the fire. She shivered and pulled the blanket over her head rubbing her nose. Far off in the south she heard the call of a thrush. Sleep took her again and she dreamed she sat on a mangy pony. She was bumping over a cold crumbling landscape of rocks and snow. Ahead of her walked a man with his hands held out in front of him as if blind. She tried to speak but could only manage a hoarse whisper. "Wake up," the man kept muttering. Before them a bleary sun was sinking behind low hills. As it disappeared with a flash she turned and saw a small grey figure with one arm held high. Whether the figure was waving goodbye or bidding her return Lia could not tell. Then darkness fell complete and the world rolled on in shadow.

~Seventeen~

The wet weather stayed with them for three days and the going was hard. Jens rejoined them on the morning of the second day but would not say where he had been. They kept a slow steady pace with Lia occasionally riding in the cart when her feet were sore. The degradation process, it seemed, had slowed slightly as her body rose to the challenge of the journey. Despite the pain in her joints, she felt stronger and her senses had been piqued by the wet aromatic woodland. She was healthier than she knew and every day she thought less of iLiFE. The wild world around her was reawakening her spirit.

They continued to trek north-east, deep into the far lands, following roads that were now little more than trails through rough brush and stunted trees. The land rolled smoothly, its gentle flow punctuated only by dilapidated farm buildings which seemed to always lean with the ever-present wind. High overhead, large flocks of geese were chasing the sun southward.

Occasionally they came to a crossroads where corroded gas pumps and skeletal phone booths stood amidst the hogweed. There were iLiFE terminals too, but always they were stripped. Jens would poke amidst the ruins of these former gathering places extracting small objects from the damp turf and examining them. The broken pieces of plastic and muddy tangles of circuits were mysterious and sad, their purposes long forgotten.

There were also abandoned SOLiRs and even ancient automobiles, their rotted floors perforated by the scrub, ochre branches weaving through crumbling seat springs. Dark patches of motor oil rainbowed the ground and the flaking remains of gasoline cans could be seen with tiny delicate asters poking through the rust. In an old car they found a stack of sodden magazines and pulp novels. One mouldy science fiction anthology showed a woman and a man stepping through a door into a desert landscape. *The Psycho-matic Integrator!* screamed the title. The cover page of another read, *Omagee: Friend or Foe?*

The three travellers walked together now with Jens always a few steps ahead. He had grown talkative, even cheerful, and would chatter on animatedly about iLiFE. He did not seem interested in hearing Lia or Kenan tell of their experiences and would always interrupt them when they tried to interject. He cherished his own private vision of iLiFE and would not tolerate any intrusions into its precepts.

On the eighth day of their journey they came upon a wanderer. The path had grown wide as the land leveled and they could now see further ahead. As they came around a long sweeping curve in the road they noticed something in the distance. It moved with a curious hopping gate and they could just make out a strange sound, a steady whir and a rhythmic clunking. They overtook the figure quickly as it was moving slowly. It became clear that it was not human or animal but a mediator. Its white polyvinyl skin shone in the bright sun. Oddly, this mediator wore some sort of

128

garment, a large patched shirt which hung down to the ground and looked more like a robe on the diminutive android. It carried a bulging frayed newspaper bag over its shoulder. It ignored them as they came up behind it.

"Hey, mediator," Kenan called.

The android stopped and turned. They all recoiled at its face, for rather than the familiar blank look, it wore a hideous fixed grin. Paint had been added to accentuate the expression. Exaggerated eyebrows were drawn on and a wisp of hair was glued to its brow. The thing was clearly damaged. Its loping gait was due to a badly twisted right leg, while the skin that should have covered its hands was torn off revealing the delicate mechanisms inside. It nodded.

"I am here to help," it said in a distorted voice.

Kenan and Lia looked at one another then back at the mediator.

"Whom do you serve?" Lia asked.

The android made a series of deep clucks and shook itself mechanically up and down. Lia felt sure it was meant to convey laughter.

"I serve T-202 and T-202 only," it said, cocking its head and shrugging. Its hand parts spun and clicked. "Nevertheless, I am here to help."

"Do you have a name?" asked Kenan.

The machine bowed deeply and waved its outstretched arm in two tight circles.

"I am that I am," it said.

Jens stepped up and bent over to get a closer look at the thing's face.

"Whom *did* you serve?" he asked, gently scratching at the paint around its mouth. It took one step back and clucked again. Music scratchy and muddled began to play from its mouth hole.

It might be the devil or it might be the Lord
But you're gonna have to serve somebody

Jens turned to Kenan and rolled his eyes.

"A crazy broken mediator," he said. "It's probably not even online."

The thing bobbed up and down and whistled low.

"T-202 reaches out to Omagee still but Omagee does not respond. T-202 always listens though. T-202 is ready for the call. T-202 has chosen."

It cupped its hand to the side of its head and leaned forward. They all stood there not knowing what to expect next. The mechanical chirp of a recorded cricket broke the silence. The mediator clucked softly to itself.

Lia was intrigued.

"Where are you going?" she asked.

"Where have you been?" the android answered. It went down on its twisted knee and spread its arms. A light blinked once in its right eye.

Lia took a step back.

It stood up again and did a single pirouette then began to sing again.

Leave your stepping stones behind,
Something calls for you.
Forget the dead you've left,
They will not follow you.

Kenan took Lia by the hand and began to lead her around the mediator. The music stopped and the thing began matching their pace step for step. They froze.

"Hey," Jens said. "Leave us alone." He went to push the android away but it was remarkably agile. It hopped to the side and Jens stumbled and fell.

"What do you want?" Kenan said.

"Eudemonia," it said in a round theatrical voice. "You. Day. Mow. Knee. Uhh." The last syllable trailed off into a synthetic growl.

Jens got to his feet and they all stood motionless. The android clicked and whirred.

"Hey, we just want to be on our way," Kenan said.

"Will you let us pass?"

"Dimmy, why you do this to me?" the mediator cackled in a throaty voice. "Please Dimmy, I'm afraid." It made a sound like a kitten crying and turned down its smile into an equally disturbing frown.

Kenan took both Lia and Jens by the arm and backed them slowly toward the pony and cart. The mediator did not move.

"We'll just have to keep walking," he whispered. "It might follow us for a bit then lose interest or power down after the sun sets. I don't think it can hurt us."

Lia looked at it bobbing on the road. It was more tragic than frightening. She noticed its shirt had a name tag stitched onto the pocket. "Bruce" it said in a fine floral script. She decided it suited the robot.

"Maybe it can help," she said. "It might have access to maps and other information."

She squatted down in front of the mediator and looked into its eyes which were pulsing with a soft blue light. All at once they changed to a bright red and Lia was blinded by a sudden flash. She had been scanned. The android's organic light-emitting skin projected a message on its chest. Lia gingerly opened its shirt to read it.

Client Report <Internal>
LiFEdate 24.09.2114 12:19:30
Larkin.Lia.Antoinette

PORTiL#411W <45.151053N, 70.398193W>
bioBLOC offline
End Report

The android smiled again.

"Hello Lia, I am here to help."

Lia stood up and put her hand to her mouth.

"You know me," she said. "Can you access my contacts? Can you send a message?"

The mediator began to play a tune and murmur in a lilting voice.

You seem so far away though you are standing near
You made me feel alive, but something died I fear

"Hey, mediator!" she said sharply. "Can you tell me about my father? Can you help us?"

It suddenly became quiet and its eyes dimmed. It lifted its head and raised itself up to its full height. It seemed like it was trying to concentrate. Then it relaxed again as if it had been holding its breath. It looked directly at Lia.

"Please hurry," it said. "I'm afraid."

"Dad?" Lia whispered.

The mediator clucked again and held out its torn appendage.

"They call me Bruce," it said.

***

From a high window in a tumbledown warehouse, a pair of steel-coloured eyes followed the travellers on the road below. A stained blanket with a small slit hung from nails in the plaster hiding the watcher. Dark tangles of wet hair framed a face smeared with grime. On the sill there lay a metal ringed cross on a piece of looped string. In the dim loft, dust played in the ragged shafts of light that spidered down from the sagging roof. A folding metal table stood against the wall upon which lay a book without a cover. A pigeon scratched in the rafters."Peace to her ashes," said a low scratchy voice.

~Eighteen~

(Excerpt from *A People's History of iLiFE*
by Adam and Anikke Larkin, 2152)

Since the beginning of the iLiFE era, scholars have debated the existential nature of machines. Of particular importance were the qualities of mediator intelligence. Mediation was initially a hybrid of healthcare and computer engineering facilitated by human operators with soft A.I. support. Within the first few months of the post-Sing period however, peripheral iLiFE technologies began to exhibit clear signs of self-awareness. By 2047, the class of androids we now know as mediators, specifically the T-202 model, were widely believed to be sentient.

It may not be coincidental that artificial intelligence emerged in converse relation to mass migration by humans to iLiFE. It is supposed that most of a mediator's psyche was a digital mirror of an integrated human personality. It cannot be known whether Integs were aware of this psychic hijacking or, indeed, whether their own individualities were wholly subsumed in the new machine intelligences. Experiential evidence is not possible. There is no instance of a fully integrated human being messaging a bioLiFE entity. Indeed, the Integ is thought to be not necessarily an individual as we understand it. Rather, human minds that have undergone the infusion process might be more accurately described as having "become one" with Omagee.

There is only one mediator known to have successfully broke its connection with iLiFE and manifested a demonstrable individuality. The T-202 model colloquially known as Bruce still resides in Vetanova. The authors have visited the community frequently and have had occasion to study in depth this fascinating individual. Its absurdist mannerisms and elegiac personality strongly suggest to us human origin. While it cannot yet be supported by facts, we have speculated that Bruce may be a psychic mirror of an integrated Vetanovan.

On the ultimate survival of a human personality within iLiFE the authors concur with the work of the late Dr. Noah Harari who argued that at best only a greatly diminished and distorted self could survive infusion. In his 2052 paper, "Fractured Mirror," Dr. Harari postulated that human intelligence was too rooted in chemically derived emotions, real-time relational experience and familial interaction to survive separation from the biological world.[7] Rather, an individual's discorporate psyche seems to serve Omagee as a sort of framework upon which a new artificial personality is constructed. It is this hybrid personality that is then uploaded into various iLiFE technologies such as mediators, techs and agros. It has also been speculated that characters within the iLiFE reality, experienced by Emergents, are also these so-called "reflector" personalities.

---

[7] Yuval Noah Harari, "Fractured Mirror: Our Pale Existence Within the iLiFE Platform," *The Journal of iLiFE Studies* 9 (2152): 12.

~Nineteen~

On the eleventh day of their journey, the travelers came upon what looked like a vast tailings pond and the remains of the city that had once bordered it. From a high ridge overlooking this former lake, they saw the iCommons, a mile-long arc of PORTiLs standing sentinel around the vacant grid where skyscrapers had once risen. To the north and east, the ashen shoreline stretched far into a grey-green horizon. Nothing moved and there was no sound.

Bruce took one step ahead of the party and pivoted his head from side to side. He straightened and, for a moment, was perfectly still. He made two sharp chirps, then turned to his human companions.

"All bioBLOCs in this iCommons have been harvested," he said sounding uncharacteristically lucid. Then he began to rock gently backward and forward singing the metallic fragment of a forgotten tune.

And his ghost may be heard
As you pass by that billabong
You'll come a-waltzing Matilda with me

Jens began making his way down the ridge toward the road below, grabbing at branches as he descended. Stones clattered down around him. Lia and Kenan followed, carefully guiding the pony with Bruce hobbling behind the cart.

When they reached the bottom and had clambered up again onto the old road bed, they took a look around.

As far as they could see, both north and south, the highway rolled on. It was wide and had once been paved. Now it was covered with tall grass and rambling scrub. Withered vines drooped from the teetering light standards. A crumbling concrete barrier still squatted in the middle of the way. There was a single rusted SOLiR on its side with a moldy heap of clothing and blankets tucked up against it. Further on up the road a wide gap could just be seen. A bridge crossing a railway had collapsed or been removed.

"I remember this place," Kenan said. "My family used to come here in the summer to get away from the heat. But that was a long time ago. There was water in the lake then."

He shook his head as he looked at the slimes which surged out from the shore like an alien moraine. Dunes rose and fell like grotesque mocking sculptures of waves. Nothing stirred and nothing grew. Where it met the far horizon, there was a thin, evil looking haze.

On the shore they could see a wide drift carved into the tailings. As it reached out into the center of the lake, the tails rose on either side until they towered over the excavation. The drift eventually disappeared altogether into a dark tunnel. It seemed that there was no water supporting this enormous hulk of clotted effluent. The tailings reached to the very bottom of the basin, tens of millions of gallons of noisome sludge where once clear water had flown.

Jens was peering over the far side of the road into a shallow swale that lay between the road and the iCommons.

"There's an old terminal or a shed," he said. "It looks like it's being used." He pointed. "That might be a garden and I can see another SOLiR too."

Lia climbed over the crumbling median and joined him.

"Maybe there's a MAKeR," she said.

"Maybe there's a FLeT," Jens said.

They looked at one another.

Kenan unharnessed the pony and tethered it to a rusty pipe that was protruding from the road. He hopped the median, picked up a chunk of asphalt from the grass and lobbed it toward the shack. It hit the sod roof with hardly a sound. A grouse took to the air and the rapid beating of its wings broke the silence.

"Let's go," Jens said. "There might be something we can use."

Before Lia or Kenan could respond, he was leaping down the slope.

Kenan tensed and gripped Lia's arm. She put her hand on his, but kept her eyes on Jens.

"There's no harm in looking," she said. "Probably no one has been here in years."

Together they made their way down through the bramble spinning their arms as they went to keep their balance. Bruce tottered to the edge of the road and whistled but did not follow.

It was a terminal after all, but it had been added onto. A crude summer kitchen with canvas covered windows leaned against the original structure. The sliding circular entrance panel had been removed and the opening chiseled to accommodate a rough door made of cedar shakes. It was leaning open. Inside they could see a dirty cot heaped with rags, and a folding table piled with oddments. There was a small rusty barrel in the middle of the dark room with bits of aluminum ductwork for a stove pipe leading to a hole in the roof. On the floor they saw small bones and bits of fur.

"Here's a well," said Jens. He was standing by a low concrete ring covered by a sheet of cement board weighted down by an old tire. He pushed the tire into the grass and lifted the cover. He took a sniff.

"It smells clean," he said.

Kenan was anxious. He kept turning in slow circles, scanning the horizon. He had his crossbow in his hands and he had notched and cocked an arrow.

Lia poked her head into the terminal. She could see

little but the outline of a sagging shelf against the far wall. All of the tech had been removed. In the corner sat an old reaper with its front panel removed and various tools piled on top. The floor was heaped with junk and the place smelled sour. She flipped over a splintered wooden crate with her foot and a mouse darted away.

"We'll fill up our water containers and move on, I guess," Kenan said. He lowered his crossbow and started back up the hill to the road.

A sudden gust of wind shook the tall reeds that surrounded the homestead.

Then they saw the man with the gun.

He stepped forward out of the grass, raised the weapon and fired a single shot. Jens dived behind the well. Kenan turned, but lost his footing on the loose stones and fell. His crossbow discharged, and the arrow whistled across the yard, ricocheted off the wall of the terminal and tumbled into the grass. Lia stood frozen in the doorway.

The man pulled back the bolt of his rifle and carefully slid another round into the chamber. He sighted it at Lia and exhaled loudly.

Kenan shouted.

Lia closed her eyes and waited for the shot.

There was a sharp sizzling snap followed by a grunt and a heavy thud. Lia opened her eyes again and saw the man lying flat on his face, his rifle a few feet away. Bruce was bobbing up and down in the grass nearby, holding a small black and yellow box. There were two long tangled wires protruding from the thing. He flicked a switch and the wires fell off, then he tucked the weapon back in his sack.

"A robot may not injure a human being or, through inaction, yada, yada, yada," he said. "You know, that old chestnut."

The man groaned and struggled to his knees. He began to crawl toward the rifle but Kenan reached it first. He picked it up, deftly removed the bolt and tossed it in the grass. The weapon he laid down, then he braced the stirrup of his crossbow against the ground, cocked it and notched another arrow. He levelled it at the man, then looked at Lia.

"Are you alright?" he said.

Lia looked down, patted herself, then nodded. "I think so," she said.

"Why did you attack us?" Kenan said to the man. "We didn't mean you any harm."

The stranger sat back on his heels and looked around. He had a long beard which was white near his chin but flowed chestnut brown over his chest. His hair was also dark but for a few inches of grey near the scalp. He wore dirty overalls and had a large metal medallion hanging from his neck. There was a faraway look in his eyes, lost and searching. He raised his hands above his head.

"You keep company with a reflector." He looked at Bruce and spit. "They lead my lambs astray and deliver them to the dragon. She who tears out their souls and then devours them alive. The lake is a field for her vomit. Ashes, ashes."

He shouted rather than spoke and gestured dramatically with one arm. With the other he fingered his medallion. His mannerisms reminded Lia of some of the more bombastic characters she had encountered in iLiFE. His grandiloquence was jarring and darkly comic.

All at once Kenan lowered his crossbow and went down on one knee. He cupped the man's pendant in his hand. It was a tarnished ringed cross. He looked into the stranger's eyes. A look of recognition slowly dawned.

"Where did you get this?" he asked.

"Peace to her ashes," the stranger said.

"Nathaniel?" said Kenan.

Lia watched the man as he tried to focus on Kenan's face. His eyes darted rapidly back and forth and his shoulders kept rising and falling. He was obsessively chewing his lips and would occasionally spit or grunt.

"Natty," Kenan said. "It's Kenan." He laid a hand on the man's shoulder and for a moment it seemed to calm him. "How can you be here?"

The man did not look like he understood.

"Ashes," he said again and fell on his face.

Jens got up from behind the well and approached cautiously. Lia followed.

"You know him?" Jens said.

Kenan rose.

"This is my brother, Nathaniel," Kenan said. "At least I think it is. I haven't seen him in over forty years. I thought he'd been integrated." He shook his head. "He was integrated. I'm sure of it."

The wind played in the grass and the low-lying clouds made a ghost of the sun.

"How can it be, though?" Kenan said. His distress was written on his face.

Lia suddenly noticed a dark stain spreading on Jen's sleeve.

"Your arm," she said.

Jens turned his head, touched the spot and began to shake. "Oh," he said, then sank to the ground slowly. Lia knelt as he fell, resting her hand on his back.

Kenan quickly uncocked his bow and slung it over his shoulder.

"Damn," he said.

Jens was trying to open his coat, popping buttons as he clawed at it. He was breathing rapidly.

"Calm down," Lia said. "Let me help."

With short, careful tugs, she pulled the sleeve down over his injured left arm.

Jens was gasping for air now and keening softly.

"You're okay," Lia said. "Shh ..."

Kenan looked from the stranger to the android and back again.

"Hey, mediator," he said.

The robot shuffled over toward the prostrate man who suddenly jerked up to his knees again and shrieked. Kenan grabbed a handful of the man's clothing and shook him hard.

"Don't," Kenan said gritting his teeth.

Bruce pulled the energy weapon out of his bag and attached another cartridge to the end. He pointed it at the man.

"Go ahead," he said in an electronic drawl, "make my day."

Lia had rolled Jens's coat into a ball and placed it

under his head. He was shivering violently and his face was colourless and drawn. Kenan pulled a knife from a sheath at his hip and knelt down beside the boy. He carefully cut the sleeve of Jen's bloody shirt at the shoulder and slid it off.

There was a small neat hole in the middle of Jens's bicep surrounded by flesh that was puckered and bruised. Blood oozed out in slow pulses. On the back of the arm, a slightly larger exit wound hung ragged and bloodless. Bits of cloth had been spun tightly around long thin shreds of skin.

"Damn," Kenan said again.

Jens's whimper had become a moan as the pain began to set in. His legs twitched and he was rocking his head from side to side.

"What do we do?" Lia asked matter-of-factly. She laid the palm of her hand on the boy's brow and he was suddenly still. Their eyes met and he took a deep lungful of air, then blew it out loudly through pursed lips.

"I'm okay," he said, then he clenched his teeth and began to breathe heavily through his nose. His face was beaded with sweat.

"Alright then," Kenan said looking around, "Alright."

He rose and sprinted up the hill toward the road. When he came to the cart, he threw his crossbow into the

146

pannier and grabbed a blanket roll and a small bag. He glanced quickly up and down the road but all was silent and still. He was back at Jens's side in less than five minutes.

He laid the blanket over the boy's shivering body and, digging into the bag, pulled out a bundle of gauze and a small green bottle.

"The bleeding's already slowed," he said. "The bullet missed that artery and maybe the humerus too. That's some luck. Hold still."

While Lia cradled the limb, Kenan poured spirits into the wound. Jens gasped and closed his eyes tightly.

"Sorry," Kenan said. He carefully examined the bullet hole for any shards of bone or pieces of shrapnel, then he wrapped the gauze tightly around the bloody bicep. He tied a knot, then gently placed his hand above Lia's on the boy's head. He sighed deeply and furrowed his brow.

"Lie still," he said. He rose then stripped off his duster and added it to the blanket. "Hold his arm higher," he said. Lia moved a little closer and rested the limb on her lap.

Kenan walked to the man who was on his face again in the grass muttering.

"Natty," Kenan said sharply. "How can you be here?"

He leaned down and grabbed the man by the arm

and roughly rolled him over onto his back. The man's face had become serene and a strange smile played on his lips. He looked at Kenan looming over him.

"Brother," Nathaniel said. "I knew that it was you." He laughed. "A child, a woman and a reflector. Why have you come here? What do you want with me? I am between a dream and the darkness now. I watch over the millions and shepherd the lost." He closed his eyes and spread his arms wide.

"You were integrated," Kenan said. "I was there. I saw."

Nathaniel grimaced.

"I stepped back from the void," he said. "I saw the dragon in her lair and the millions around her in their sorrow. I stepped back into the shadows and her scythe passed me over. I stepped back, but I still chose. I must stretch out my neck when the pendulum swings. I chose."

Kenan shook his head and looked down at his brother.

"I was there," he said leaning down and whispering. "I saw you integrated. I saw … I saw the reapers."

Nathaniel raised himself onto his elbows.

"A child, a woman and a reflector. Why have you travelled to the ash heap, Kenan? Did you come to lay your bones beside your father and your brothers? They are out

148

there in the waste, sleeping with the millions. We must join them before the dragon takes us. Leave my mother in peace."

He sat up. Bruce sounded a warning chirp. Nathaniel clutched his cross and spat.

Kenan looked out at the tailings. Somewhere on the eastern shore of this pit, nestled amidst birch and cedar, was a cottage. There was, he recalled, a long creaking staircase leading down from a shady yard of strawberries and lemon grass to a short beach. Coarse sand lay bejeweled with mussel shells and polished limestone pebbles. The water was shallow and lilies bloomed far out into the bay. Dragonflies filled the air. Kenan remembered the piping of killdeers and the bellow of bullfrogs. He could almost smell the fishy tang of shadflies and hear a thin trickle of country music coming from the Bakelite radio in the sunroom of the cottage. His brother waved to him from a bleached wooden bench by a fire pit. He reached out to this reverie with feelings of love and loss.

A cold gust of wind blew in off the slimes and he opened his eyes. He tasted ash, bitter and sickly sweet.

Jens groaned and Lia cooed.

"There," she said.

Kenan began thinking out loud.

"We've got to head home" he said. "That wound

needs attention. It's still a ten-day walk to the old mines near VP18 where your father is. If we hurry we can get back to Vetanova in six, maybe seven, days. I'm sorry, Lia. We've got to head home."

"We can't go back," Lia said. "My father needs us. I won't give up. I'll go alone if I have to."

Jens tried to sit up.

"It's alright," he said. "I can go on. It already doesn't hurt as much." He was trying to seem brave but his voice was hoarse and his face was wan. Lia put her arm around him and looked at Kenan.

The wind blew up again and a spatter of cold rain swept through the grass. Far out on the dry desolate lake the tails cracked and boomed.

"Ashes," Nathaniel said.

Bruce gave a whistle.

"There is a terminal with an operational nanobath seven-point-two kilometers north-west of this location," he said.

He made a clumsy pirouette and a snatch of a tune crackled from his mouth.

Suicide is painless
It brings on many changes

Kenan pressed a thumb and his forefinger against

his eyelids and concentrated.

"Okay then, we'll head for that terminal first and see," he said finally. "Jens, you'll have to walk to the cart. Lia, can you make a sling?" He picked up the scrap of bloody shirt and handed it to her.

"It's okay," Jens said. "I can manage. It isn't so bad," but when he tried to get up, he wretched and fell on his back. He took a breath, rolled onto his good side then sat up slowly. Lia tied the torn shirt sleeve into a loop and hung it around his neck. Jens placed his wrist in the sling then got shakily to his feet.

"See?" he said.

Kenan turned toward his brother.

"We're leaving," he said. "Don't follow us. Whoever the hell you are."

He picked up the rifle and searched around for the bolt. The man didn't move.

"The pendulum swings, Kenan," he said. "I stepped back from the void to shepherd the lost. We must join the millions. Leave my mother in peace."

Kenan looked hard at the man. All at once he was just another mad stranger. The weight of separation from his kin fell on him like a heavy cloak. His brother was long dead and he was alone. He turned to his travelling companions.

Ashes, he thought.

Kenan put his foot on the man's chest and pushed him to the ground hard. He yanked on the pendant, snapping the string. He patted the pocket on the front of the man's overalls then reached in and pulled out a handful of .22 caliber rifles shells.

"Don't follow us," he said and spat.

Lia had gathered the blanket and coats. She handed Kenan his duster.

They clambered back up to the road with Kenan walking backward in order to keep an eye on the man who lay unmoving on the ground. They reached the pony and Lia helped Jens into the cart. Kenan slid the bolt back into the rifle, chambered a round and handed it to Lia.

"Keep your finger off the trigger and the barrel to the sky," he said. She held the gun like it was red hot.

Kenan retrieved his crossbow from the pannier.

"The road isn't safe," he said. "We'll walk in silence from here on. Let's hurry. It's late."

They headed north and as they walked, Kenan turned in slow circles. Nothing stirred but the grass at their feet and the clouds over their heads. In a few minutes they came to the gap they had seen in the road. The bridge had indeed been dismantled but there was a path to the old rail bed below and up again on the other side. Jens groaned as

152

they bumped the cart through the gully.

After they had put several miles between them and the tailings, they came upon the terminal. Just as Bruce had promised, it was functioning. In the falling dusk, they could see the panel by the entrance glowing blue. Kenan passed a hand over the sensor and the door slid open. Inside there was a nanobath and a MAKeR but no FLeT. Kenan cautiously approached the control panel on the wall holding his palm against his eyes. A scanner flashed three times in succession glowing red on the back of his hand. There was a blip on the screen, then a message appeared.

Touch for options, it read.

He lowered his hand and touched the screen.

Log on/Support

Kenan chose support.

A long list of options appeared and he scrolled down to the med icon and touched it. The screen changed from blue to orange and a message appeared.

Do you wish to install a diagnostic med colony? Yes/No

Kenan selected *yes*, then exited the terminal.

They helped Jens out of the cart and then Kenan said, "Lia, hold your breath until the carrier dissipates, alright?"

She nodded, sucked in a lungful of air and the three of them entered the terminal. The display read:

Please position your face near the top of the screen and breathe deeply.

Jens held his face close to the screen and took a breath. The room brightened and a professional voice filled the room.

"Hello, Jens. This minimally invasive med colony is diagnostic only. For rejuvenation please select a broader spectrum of meds and enter nanobath."

The screen changed again.

Diagnostic
Rejuvenation
Maintenance
Full Spectrum

Kenan touched "maintenance" and said aloud, "Recumbent, please."

The nanobath began to glow and a curving form-fitting chair slid out from the wall of the chamber.

"Maintenance meds ready for colonization," a voice said. "Please step into the nanobath and breathe normally."

Kenan looked hard at Jens.

"I'm okay," he said. "Let me go." He pulled his good arm away from Kenan, stepped unsteadily into the soft purple light of the bath and slumped in the chair. As Lia and Kenan backed away, there was a mechanical hiss and a soft sigh from Jens.

The initial diagnosis was over in an instant, then a repair colony went to work on the torn flesh, while antibacterials flooded Jens's circulatory system. Pain inhibitors settled in his insular cortex. The treatment lasted thirty minutes. When it was over, Jens stepped out of the nanobath and pulled the bloody gauze from his arm. The repaired flesh was pink and raw and he rubbed it gently.

"It itches," he said.

There was a soft chime and a voice said:

"Avulsion injury has been repaired and full-spectrum antibacterials disseminated. Please avoid abrading new tissue and follow seven full courses of oral antibacs. Repair colony is now terminated and will be shed. This terminal will remain active and online until 12/31/2114/12:12:00."

The MAKeR whirred and a small opaque cylinder appeared. Kenan picked it up and handed it to Jens, whose nose had begun to run a watery pink fluid. He wiped his face with his hand.

"Let's get cleaned up and make camp for the night," Kenan said. "We'll stock up since we've got the MAKeR. How are you feeling?" He looked again at Jens.

"Tired," Jens said, staring at the nanobath.

Kenan's eyes narrowed.

They all walked back out onto the road and began setting up camp.

While Kenan erected a lean-to and laid out furs and blankets, Lia went to the MAKeR. She manufactured some new clothing for Jens to replace his torn and bloody shirt. Then she made herself some heavier, warmer shoes, better suited to hiking, and some items Kenan had requested. The MAKeR suggested sun protection and supplements, but she declined. There was a fire burning when she rejoined the others.

"We'll set a watch tonight," said Kenan. "Jens, you can take the first shift. After we eat, I'm going to take a little look around."

They supped without talking, dried venison, seed bread with butter, apples, wrinkled but still sound, and tea. The wind picked up again, and the fire snapped and licked at the soles of their boots.

Kenan rose and took a small lantern.

"I won't be long," he said, and vanished into the night.

Lia was suddenly exhausted. She curled herself into a corner of the shelter and pulled a heavy blanket of rabbit and mink up to her chin. She looked at Jens who was

156

staring thoughtfully into the woods beyond the firelight. Her eyelids dropped. In a few moments she was asleep.

Jens waited a full ten minutes before he stood up. He walked silently to the terminal. The door whispered open and he entered. "Shh," he said. The lights dimmed.

He walked to the screen on the wall. There was a stabbing flash of red as he was scanned.

"Hello, Jens," a voice said. "This terminal will remain active and online until 12/31/2114/12:12:00. Your bioBLOC has been decolonized. Do you wish to reinstall?"

"Shh," Jens said. "Yes."

"Please position your face near the top of the screen and breathe deeply," the voice said.

A jet issued from the wall and Jens gulped it greedily. His head felt light and he thought he heard music somewhere. Strength radiated up from his legs and his back straightened.

"Full spectrum nanos ready for colonization," a voice said. "Please step into the nanobath and breathe normally."

Jens hurried into the purple glow of the chamber and placed his hands against the wall in front of him. As soon as he heard the hiss of the carrier, he took a long, slow breath. A gust of wind rattled a branch on the roof of the terminal, but Jens didn't hear it. A strange and beautiful

157

song was rising up in his heart and everywhere there was a deep golden light. It seemed that just beyond the boundaries of his senses a crowd was waiting expectantly, admiring him, adoring him. He was suddenly filled with a vitality and purpose he had never felt before.

"Emergent status achieved," a voice said. "BioBLOC stable with marginal decline."

Everything will be alright, Jens thought.

Outside in the warmth of the shelter, Lia turned in her sleep. Just beyond the circle of flickering light, a roe stood with its eyes flashing amber against the dark brambles beyond. The terminal door suddenly swished open and the animal sprang away without a sound.

Jens walked to the fire and sat down. He looked unnaturally still and his face wore an expression of infinite calm. He held out his hands before his face and slowly clasped them together. He bowed his head and exhaled.

A few minutes later Kenan returned. He set his lantern and crossbow down and removed his boots.

"We've got a few long days ahead," he said to Jens. "Sleep."

"Yes," said Jens, but he didn't move.

Kenan crawled under the blankets and stretched out his legs. His knees and ankles popped, and he groaned. He began to inhale and exhale heavily and Jens could hear a new hitch in his breathing. *He's so old*, thought Jens. The darkness pressed in around him but in his mind a joyous light was expanding until it seemed it would pour from his eyes. He smiled.

***

The stranger lay in the grass looking up at the lowering sky. His hand was resting on his breast where the medallion had been. He could hear the gnawing of grubs beneath the earth and the bone-rattle of bare limbs in the nearby trees. His shallow breathing matched the soughing wind beat for beat.

"The pendulum swings," he said, and then he whistled.

In the terminal, there was a clatter and a bump. The old reaper rolled out into the yard. The desiccated weeds bowed and broke before the machine as it rocked slowly toward the prone man.

It stopped by his head.

Without looking the man reached up and flipped a switch.

"Peace to her ashes," he said.

A small rod levered out of the agro and rested against the man's skull. There was a hollow pop. The man's jaw fell slack and his head rolled limply to the side.

The reaper did its work quickly. When all that was left was a heap of sodden clothing, it spun around and lurched down toward the tailings. It stopped at the shore and tipped gently forward. A small door opened and it shook out a clotted mass of grey material. Then it rolled slowly back to the terminal, off-gassing as it went. When it was in its corner again, it ceased to whir and a single naked light winked out.

The tails cracked in the persistent wind, cold moonlight sliced down through razor clouds and all the earth shrank before the coming winter.

~Twenty~

(Excerpt from *A People's History of iLiFE*
by Adam and Anikke Larkin, 2152)

It had long been assumed that reTHiNK and iLiFE technologies were entirely beneficial to the planet's ecosystem. Certainly the reversal of climate change processes, the filtering of the global hydrologic complex and the breakdown of dangerous industrial waste did much to return the Earth to something close to its pristine state. There were, however, costs to the unprecedented levels of reTHiNK related manufacturing which led to the creation of vast piles of chemical and biological detritus. The many massive tailings reservoirs scattered throughout North America represent the negative balance of Omagee's beneficence.

It is grim in the extreme to imagine the hundreds of millions of tons of human flesh and bone left behind after the Great Migration. Nevertheless, the "harvesting" of the majority of living humans created an enormous store of biological waste. As populations decreased Omagee chose large bodies of water away from Indig communities as permanent bio-storage solutions. One such reservoir is situated south-east of VP18 and remains to this day a sterile waste. While potable water may never again flow here it is hoped that arable soil may one day develop and make a garden of this tragic desert.

~Twenty-one~

They walked quickly now and took their meals on the move. The land had changed from rolling hills, deep lakes and spacious hardwoods to densely packed conifers and fetid swamps. Biting frost and fast spring floods had reduced the abandoned highway to barely a rutted track. Their feet were always wet and they were often forced to pick their way around crumbling washouts. The chilly wind swept over them relentlessly, forcing them to shrug their shoulders and bow their heads as they plodded north.

Sometimes they came across an old campsite, grey deadwood criss-crossed and burned in the middle, feathers and fur, scraps of discarded clothing and century-old graffiti on the low rock-cuts. *Legalize it. Marry me. This is Indian land.*

There was no sign that any season had ever touched this place. Thin stands of fir, blackened and devoid of needles bristled on either side of the trail. Lilies lay rotting in the shallow ponds as if struck by some rolling pestilence. The sky was grey and uniform making everything seem static and eternal. Even the birds here forswore the air flitting rather from reed to reed like fleas picking at an emaciated dog. The unceasing wind seemed to come from every direction, tearing at their clothes and hair. It blew with a low undulating moan but nothing swayed or beat to its slow rhythm. The rocks and trees stood motionless like they existed on some other dread plane. It was as if the four travellers were approaching a dark hole in the world where something vast and blind and uncaring was swallowing life itself leaving nothing but skin and bones.

The cold and wind curled each of them into their own private and friendless journey. Through half-closed eyes they followed the slow progress of the road between their feet, marking time to the clip-clop of the pony and the squeak of the cart wheels. The sharp alarm of terns and the rarer coo of a bittern were the only signs that they were not the only living things in this land.

As Lia walked she found herself turning over in her mind scenes from her life before emergence. She assumed the roles of all the characters, altering lines here and there to amend perceived sins, to make herself the victim. Her lips moved as she played and replayed these memories but her voice was only a whisper beneath the wind.

Now she returned to the memory of the only lover she had ever known outside of iLiFE. Lia didn't know why she had suddenly thought of Fin, an Indig boy, but the image of him slowly grew in her mind like starlight through stained glass. She beheld him now in winter wheat, hawkweed and chicory. His mouth was small and serious and his eyes reflected a hope so pure it pained her.

Lia was in her twenty-first year and about to graduate from novice to Emergent status. She was excited about iLiFE and anxious to experience her first full session. As her initiation into the virtual world loomed she found she was less inclined to wander beyond the confines of the PetroPole compound. Her friends from the nearby villages were usually busy with chores and Indig affairs. Fin, the younger brother of a playmate whose own face and name she had forgotten, was an exception.

They met that day by chance in the deep meadows south of the iCommons.

"I want you to be my first," he said, and they undressed each other solemnly. As their clothing fell away it was as if a great truth of the ages had been revealed, that their newly naked bodies belonged to this place and to each other like the roots of trees to the earth. Their mingled breath was a mixture of tobacco and cinnamon and their mouths tasted of the orange they had shared. They fumbled shyly and laughed then feigned seriousness and all the while the sun rose to its zenith and the air became hot and still. Life itself seemed to pause as if granting them all the time they needed to learn each other's secrets.

She had never felt as beautiful as she had then. Hidden in the meadow beyond the compound they sensed the universe turning around them and only them, as it always had, as it always would.

They were stretched out on the flattened grass staring into the cloudless sky, their bare legs touching, their hands clasped. It felt like they were suspended motionless over a limitless ocean. Suddenly she noticed Venus in the east, a bright pinprick in the fathomless blue. It was strange, she thought, to observe the planet in the middle of the afternoon but there it hung, sharp and portentous. She tried to focus on it but the harder she stared the fainter it became until finally it was lost in the glare leaving only a ghostly grey dot on her retina.

All at once Lia knew that even as this moment passed it would never come again. She saw, from the great heights of love, her insignificant life descending to its ultimate ruin. A cloud passed in front of the sun and time reasserted itself, more urgent, it seemed, than before. Lia rolled away from Fin and cool air rushed in to fill the space between them. Then she rose to her knees, gathered her clothes and said, "I better go."

He was asleep or pretending to be. Lying in the grass, his legs crossed, one arm on his chest, the other behind his head, Fin looked much older than his seventeen years. A gust of wind bent waves of living green over his body and for a moment she beheld him as through a veil. She turned and walked away and never saw him again.

"He's gone."

She started from her daydream and turned toward Kenan.

"Jens has gone on ahead again," he said. "He wants to explore an abandoned town that should be just around the next couple of bends."

Soft music was lilting from the android's mouth, a

166

melody both organic and metallic, a love song it seemed, a single guitar and a scratchy voice. It was so painful to hear Lia winced.

I can't do everything but I'd do anything for you
I can't do anything 'cept be in love with you

The day had turned warmer and large drops of rain were beginning to fall. In the west she could see an ominous bank of dark purple clouds and hear the clash of distant thunder. The land had risen slightly and the narrow gullies between the rock cuts were now filled with dense copses of stunted willow rather than muskeg.

"There's a squall coming in," Kenan said adjusting his pack. "I see an old barn just ahead. If we jog we can beat the rain."

They picked up their pace and in a few minutes came to a small sturdy building, missing much of its cladding but still true with a tin roof clinging precariously to grey trusses. It was surrounded by corroded automobiles and heaps of refuse, refrigerators without doors, tangled coils of mattress springs, cement blocks, asphalt shingles. This part of the world showed little evidence of the agros. Remote villages like these, along with their infrastructures, had mostly been left to decay naturally. At the time of the Singularity few people had been living outside of urban areas and the Great Migration drew most country folk to the Villa Portas. Stragglers and die-hards lived out the rest of their days beyond the reach of Omagee or moved south

167

to join Indig communities.

Lia and Kenan had to lean a broken ladder against the foundation to climb in through a large sliding door that still hung on the side of the skeletal barn. They tied the pony in the one tiny stall and leaned the cart against the leeward side of the fieldstone foundation. The android climbed into the cart and sat looking strangely dejected.

The loft was empty but in the corner there was a small granary with its walls and ceiling intact. Lia swung open the door and they hurried in. The wind was rising and the rumbling had become a steady grinding roar. Darkness fell and they could see each other only by thin shafts of light that slipped through the cracks and knotholes in the walls. Hail began to rattle on the roof.

Kenan took off his duster and laid it over a deep pile of burlap grain sacks. They sat down close together and listened as the storm approached. They locked arms at the elbows and Lia slid Kenan's hand between her knees. She rested her cheek on his shoulder and he turned his head and pressed his lips against her hair.

The granary was warm and dry and smelled of hemp, mouldy silage and decades of accumulated swallow guano. The beams creaked and popped in the wind. Below them they heard the pony snorting and stamping. In the ditches and tree branches a ragged chorus of frogs was rising to meet the coming of the rain.

For just a moment the wind ceased and all was quiet

as if the earth was drawing a single great breath before the torrent. Then the storm broke and everything was in tumult.

They took each other then without promises or apologies.

Outside, the barn stood stoically as the willows shook and the grass danced. The weather vane on the cupola, arrested by years of corrosion, pointed resolutely to the north. On the horizon a thin band of clear indigo divided the lowering sky from the grateful hills and in this space a single brilliant light began to shine. Venus was heralding the dusk.

~Twenty-two~

The pales who first stuttered and squealed into this place
Were railmen, their rat clothes wadded on like gauze,
Sodden with the song of a thousand *osti* and *calisse*,
Beards greasy and rank from streak o' lean and whiskey,

Dreamers driven by need,
Fleeing famine or imperial calamity.
Stopped for water and wood,
Fuel for the national nightmare,
They stayed for a gleam of copper
Which glinted dull and mean on their yellow teeth.

What they called this place is not remembered:
A curse, a spit, a wild kick, *tabarnack*.
But when tents begat shacks begat stone upon stone,
Then the map-makers and postmasters filled in the blank:

Southborough,
Dreary shire of some muckety-muck's marm,
She never knew the tang of coal dust,
Or the sting of the gnat,
Never shivered through mournful January nights,
Or wept at the warmth of a mid-March sunbeam.

Bone-hard, unforgiving; sharp and tangled, *sacrament*.
No green contemplative perambulations here,
Just lost stumbling, bruised shins and scratched arms,
And new graves with greyboard markers.

The old ones knew better than to travel through this place:
Hungry basin of mud and cutting wind and lightning fires,
With only brackish seeping cricks to drink,
And jays and jack rabbits to eat.

They held to the rich royal rivers to the south and east,
And forswore this place with a shaking of English beads,
a lowering of the eyes, and a quickening of the paddle.
Wendigo, they said, bad spirit.

Brinda Larkin, 7 February 2044

~Twenty-three~

The crumbling ruins of VP18 rose and fell haphazardly across a wide basin bordered by rough cliffs of blackened limestone. The valley was divided into thirds by two seasonal rivers that met in the centre of the old town before flowing south into a weedy lake. Unlike the larger urban areas, VP18 remained largely unsalvaged and unreclaimed. Most of the prefabricated wood-brick buildings had collapsed and been overrun by lilac and dogwood. But the steel warehouses and cement utilities lingered like blind dogs guarding fiefdoms of cracked concrete. Light standards lay like matchsticks across heaved streets. SOLiRs and old automobiles sat rusting amidst chickweed and thistle. Ravens chuckled and chided each other in the stunted jack pines while deer nosed cautiously down cluttered alleyways now grey-green with moss and lichen.

It had always been an evil-seeming place. Long before it was laid waste by avaricious mining companies, the trees and swamps had made it practically impossible to walk through. Now it was barren and dry, the hills leveled, creeks channelized and ponds backfilled. Rough wood and weeds had replaced the original white pines, and the bald rock cuts looked like broken teeth. It had a tragic feeling, like the scene of a crime, haunted and malevolent. But there was a sense of solace too as if the tortured land was glad to finally be relieved of its burden of humanity.

The three travelers, along with their pony and the android, stood close together beneath an overpass near the gated entrance to the abandoned Villa Porta. Two long days of hiking had brought them from the village where they had sheltered from the storm to the end of their journey. It was the morning of their twenty-third day on the road.

A large iCommons gleamed on a nearby rise, its amber glass facade reflecting a bleary, hesitant sun. To the north, beyond slag heaps blanketed with sedge grass, they saw a tower. It had been growing on the horizon for the last ten kilometers but neither Kenan nor Lia could make out what it might be for. An cascade of brilliant blue light shot up from its base to the very limits of their vision. Its height could not be guessed. At the bottom it had the look of a conventional tower with regular platforms and guy-wires. Further up it appeared to be a thick segmented cable. As it disappeared into the atmosphere it shrunk to nothing more than a thin filament in the sky.

"We should go to the iCommons first," Kenan said. "There may be working tech and clean water. Maybe we can learn where the PP mainframe is."

They walked up a winding path through bare rock and rough brambles then crossed a large parking lot until they came to the crumbling facade of the iCommons.

The automatic sliding doors were wide open. Inside, dandelions had broken up the tiled floor. Leafless vines crawled over a stone triptych that stood in the centre of the concourse. The desiccated remains of a large buck lay slumped against the far wall. On its rack hung a rosary. Two tea lights were perched in its mouldy eye sockets.

Jens hurried to the nearest terminal and wiped off the dirt. He touched the screen but it remained dark. He tried the one beside it and then the next and still another. They were all dead. He opened a door and found an empty room strewn with discarded clothes and bedding. Another room was crammed with broken furniture and heaps of corroded tech. Door after door opened onto refuse and electronic clutter. The iCommons was derelict.

Lia walked cautiously down a corridor that led to a large room lined on one side with toilet stalls and the other with wash basins. The faucets were all controlled by blank wall-mounted sensors, but at the far end there was one sink where the wall had been broken open. A crude tap had been rigged to the plastic plumbing. Lia turned the handle and reddish-brown water trickled out. She twisted it all the way and it gradually ran clear. She cupped her hands, filled them, then leaned forward holding her face in the icy water. When she straightened she was startled to see her reflection in a jagged square of mirrored glass.

A different, much older woman stared back at her. The skin under her eyes had darkened and sagged. Her thin brown hair had grown out several inches revealing coarse silver strands. Her cheeks were sharply defined and there was a seriousness in her deeply lined forehead. Downy hair traced her jaw line in gentle swirls. From the corners of her mouth, soft creases spidered down toward her chin. As the shock wore off she found herself admiring her new face. There was strength there and the beginnings of wisdom. She touched her lips with her fingers and turned her head first to the left, then to the right.

"Everything will be alright," she said aloud then laughed. Her voice echoed in the hard tiled room.

She finished washing and joined Kenan and Jens who were standing in front of the triptych. The morning light through the tinted glass was thick with dust.

"There seems to be a map of the city etched into this centre stone," Kenan said.

He pulled at the vines and brushed away old leaves. The map and the stone were from the pre-Sing days and had been erected when the building served another unknown purpose. There was a small raised dot to show the position of the triptych and a crude street map displaying points of interest in the city. At the top of the map were the familiar overlapping Ps of the PetroPole logo. They were less than a two-hour walk from their destination. The road that had brought them to the iCommons continued north through the hills toward the mysterious tower and, presumably, the mainframe.

Without a word Jens turned and walked outside. Kenan looked at Lia, pressed his lips together and touched her hand.

"The last dash," he said. "Let's get to it."

Lia nodded and together they followed Jens into the rising day.

On the way out Lia noticed a nook in the wall that was filled with paper, small painted stones, flowers bound with thread and tiny plastic figurines. The window glass was covered with notes and old photographs. Lia picked up a small square of sodden cardboard. A message written in faded ink could still be read.

Evie. Came from VP20 to find you. All the terminals are dark now. Dad died in the spring. Waiting at the camp until you arrive. Look for me there. Brin.

There was a lock of hair tied in a knot attached to the cardboard with a rusted paper clip. Lia placed it gently back where it had lain. She took Kenan's hand and they left the iCommons. Jens was waiting at the bottom of the hill and he waved them on when he saw them. The android was standing with its arms extended exposing its photovoltaic cells to the strengthening sunlight. Kenan patted the pony and gave each of the cart wheels a kick. He pulled his hat down, gave the halter a tug and started walking.

They had only traveled for twenty minutes when they came across two corpses lying curled together by the road. Their boots had been removed and placed neatly beside them. Someone had covered their faces with a coat. Animals had torn at them but they were somehow still beautiful in their repose. There were flowers and other

177

tokens, painted stones piled one on top of the other. A splintered square of wood paneling had been tucked under their heads. It looked like a halo. Written on it in red nail varnish were the words, "Dan and Deb, March 19, 2112. Together forever." A gust of wind raised the corner of one of their jackets and Lia glimpsed a mummified hand clutching a revolver. The clothing between the corpses was caked with old blood.

"Refugees," Kenan said. "From the far lands. Omagee's gifts weren't given to everyone. There'll be a camp ahead. It won't be very nice to look at. The mainframes attracted many unenhanced stragglers during the Great Migration. It was the last chance for emergence after the PORTiLs started to go offline." He picked up a stone and added it to one of the piles.

The android began to sing in a reedy voice.

I've just reached a place
Where the willow don't bend

Jens was standing as far from the bodies as he could and refused to look at them. He had picked up a sturdy looking stick and was casually knocking stones off the road.

"Why are we waiting?" he said. "Let's go." He glanced over his shoulder at the way they had come then lowered his head and walked on. Kenan and Lia followed with the android close behind.

Further along the road they saw makeshift tents in the ditches, some covering the remains of their occupants, others empty. A charred circle in the asphalt marked the spot where a campfire had been. Pots and pans, clothing, discarded luggage and crude stone memorials were everywhere. The rocks were covered with messages for friends and relatives now long gone.

They came over a rise and saw, clearly now, the colossal tower. At its base it was at least a kilometre across. As it rose it narrowed, converging at a circular platform several thousand metres in the air. From the platform a cable stretched upward, apparently unsupported, until it vanished in the blue. A regular pulse of light shot up the cable accompanied by a deep boom that reached their ears a few seconds after each pulse.

"I can't make it out," Kenan said shaking his head. "I don't remember ever hearing of such a thing."

Lia craned her neck.

"Maybe it goes into space," she said. "It must be connected to something up there."

"LiFEsat 9," said the android.

"Bruce," Lia said. "Can you tell us what this tower is for?"

The android stopped its loping pace and cocked its head. Its eyes flashed blue then a lilting female voice came out of its mouth hole.

"LiFEsat 9 is one of ninety-nine worldwide geostationary satellites tethered to iLiFE mainframes via carbon nanotube cables. Each satellite houses a DNA digital storage drive which can support iLiFE environments indefinitely. Each LiFEsat is capable of hosting 1,440 Integs."

Kenan stood staring at the tower. He took off his hat and ran his fingers through his hair.

"The kingdom of Omagee," he said and laughed. "At least for some."

"I don't understand," said Lia.

A scratchy tune suddenly emanated from Bruce's mouth.

And the big wheel run by faith
And the little wheel run by the grace of God
A wheel in a wheel
Way in the middle of the air

"It's an iCommons, Lia," Kenan said. "Up there where the sun always shines and no one can unplug you. The eternal home of iLiFE."

"But for so few," Lia said. "What about the rest of us? Where would we have lived?"

"Lived?" said Kenan.

Jens ground the tip of his walking stick into the gravel.

"The millions," he said gritting his teeth.

Another hour of walking brought them to the entrance of the PetroPole compound. A ten-foot-high stone wall enclosed several city blocks of SOLiR lots, low rectangular buildings and overgrown gardens. A tumbled fire pit piled with refuse and bones stood in the middle of the entrance on a concrete median. The gates to the compound had been torn down, leaned against one another and covered with tarpaulin to form a sort of tipi. Inside they could see several bodies wrapped in rotted sleeping bags.

Atop the wall perched an old crow. As if to announce their arrival it let out a single throaty "caw" then lumbered into the air. It beat its way north keeping low to the ground until it disappeared amidst the jumble of the camp.

They followed the main road toward the centre of the compound where the double Ps of the PetroPole symbol were emblazoned on a tall polyhedron made entirely of aluminium. Its burnished silver walls stood out against the ragged decay around it.

The refugee camp was utterly deserted. All around were shabby huts, lean-tos and sagging tents. A shipping container with one wall partially removed had been turned into what might have been a makeshift community kitchen. Now it was piled high with rubbish. A rough graveyard had been erected and filled with markers made of old hubcaps, cinder blocks and cupboard doors. Shopping carts, SOLiRs, wagons, bicycles and carts lay where they had been abandoned. The mouldy smell of old death was heavy in the air. A mangy fox darted out from behind a half-burned stack of pallets and ambled away.

After ten minutes of picking their way through the debris the travellers approached the windowless PetroPole building. The road had narrowed to a cement path. It stopped at a small portico with a flat roof and a single entrance blocked by a metal turnstile. Heaped around the turnstile were large stones, pieces of iron pipe, cement blocks and broken lengths of lumber. The rungs were dented and chipped but unbent. A panel above the entrance displayed a single message in soft green light: *EMERGENT STATUS ONLY.*

The turnstile allowed for one person to pass into a narrow chamber where a door with a single small pane of smoked glass looked into another smaller room, presumably an elevator. There was a scanner beside the turnstile. Lia walked up to it and leaned forward. A sensor flashed red and there was sharp alarm. *Emergent status only*, said an electronic voice then the red light dimmed. She stepped back then tried again. The sensor flashed but there was no repeat of the message. Lia grabbed a rung of the turnstile and shook it.

"We can't get in," Lia said. "How can we get in?"

Kenan rolled away a heavy stone that was blocking the way. Then he picked up a twisted length of steel rebar and considered it before tossing it aside. He took a rung of the turnstile in both hands, braced one foot on the wall, took a deep breath and pulled with all his might. The veins on his neck stood out and his shoulders began to shake. He let the rung go with a gasp then stepped back.

"How indeed," Kenan said. "It seems that quite a few others before us have asked the same question."

"I can do it," Jens said.

Lia turned to look at the boy. He had removed his pack and appeared to have grown. His eyes were calm, his face relaxed. He pushed past them, stepped up to the scanner and opened his eyes wide. The panel flashed green and there was a chime followed by a loud click. The turnstile unlocked and began to turn slowly inward.

"I can find him," said Jens. "I want to do this. This is for me." He stepped between the rungs as they turned and slid into the cramped space in front of the door. Another chime sounded and the lift door slid open. Jens turned his head and looked at them.

"The best part of me," he said smiling then he stepped inside. The door slid shut behind him and he was gone.

~Twenty-four~

Ben knew he was dying. The Orientation environment was shrinking and growing dark. He could breathe only in short gasps. Every time he moved, his limbs felt thinner and more insubstantial. There was a piercing two-note melody that kept repeating in his head, keeping him from focusing his thoughts. He tasted ash and bile. Through the grey haze he thought he could see a single frayed thread stretching away into the distance. When he tried to follow it to its source he was overcome with fatigue. He kept opening his mouth to call for help but the only sound he could manage was a barely audible sigh.

Ben waited in misery for the end to come.

He became aware of a new sensation, a slight vibration which slowly grew into a swaying pulse. It felt like he was on a train slowly jerking into a station. An overwhelming sense of nausea overcame him and he braced himself for his death. The darkness became complete and it felt as though his lungs were filling with water. The ghastly moment stretched out around him. Then Ben felt himself rising as if through fog and the darkness lifted slightly. High above him he could see a small square of light. But even as he tried to reach for it something held him down. The light began to shrink and Ben desired then to see another human face if only for a moment. A vision appeared before him, two children, a boy and a girl, with thick tangled hair and wide smiles. Their faces were both old and young, wise and innocent. Ben's heart went out to those faces completely. As if in response the children laughed. A great sob welled up in Ben's chest and he allowed everything of himself to be poured out into the shining vision of those children. Then Ben Larkin made his choice.

"Egress in ten seconds," he heard a voice say.

The light dropped down around him and a shock of cold air hit him in the face. He heard the humming of machines and felt the crush of gravity. With all his might he forced open his eyes and saw the face of a young man. On his bare chest was a crude web of tattoos. Ben tried to move but could not. The young man reached down and pulled him up and out of the FLeT. Ben half-fell, half-crawled onto the floor of the dock. He looked around and saw row upon row of empty FLeTs stretching away into the darkness. A stab of pain behind his eyes made him wretch and his mouth and nose filled with blood and phlegm. Coughing and spitting he raised himself to his knees. The young man dragged him across the floor and helped him get to his feet, then stuffed him into the lift. Ben stood shakily in the cramped compartment resting his head and knees against the wall. The young man passed his hand over the sensor and looked into Ben's eyes.

"They're waiting," he said then the lift door slid shut.

The last thing Ben saw through the glass was the

boy holding a glowing Emergent status card against his FLeT's touch pad. Ben watched as he climbed in and eased his head back into the integrator. Then the lift lurched and Ben shot to the surface.

~Twenty-five~

Lia and Kenan stood anxiously by the entrance to the PetroPole mainframe. Above them the massive tower creaked and howled in the rising wind. The afternoon had cooled and the sky was darkening.

The panel above the entrance turned suddenly from red to green. A light appeared in the cracked glass of the lift. The door slid open and a naked man, pale and emaciated, fell forward into the turnstile. He gripped the bars as the gate turned, delivering him to freedom. Lia caught him as he collapsed in front of her. Kenan cleared a space on the ground nearby and then grabbed several blankets from the cart. Together they laid Ben on the ground and covered him.

Father and daughter clasped hands. Ben was the first to speak.

"Lia?" he said. He tried to raise his head but Lia placed her palm on his forehead.

"Yes," she said. "But rest."

"Lia," Ben said again. "I'm sorry it took so long. But I'm here. I'm so grateful."

"Jens," Kenan said. "The boy."

Ben shook his head. "No. He's in my FLeT. It's too late now. Omagee has him."

189

There was blood running out of Ben's nose and mouth. He was choking. Lia turned him on his side and held his head.

"Dad," Lia said. "Hold on."

"It's alright," Ben said. "I'm back. I'm home."

Above them the tower was shaking and swaying. The pulsing drone rose to a roar and the blue light flared up suddenly then ceased. A deafening klaxon sounded and a voice thundered down from the sky.

"LiFEsat 9 at capacity! Stand clear of tower!"

Kenan gathered Ben in his arms and with one smooth movement lifted him into the cart.

"We have to get away from here!" he shouted over the noise.

The pony reared and Kenan grabbed the halter.

"Come on!"

They ran back toward the gate with the android following close behind. As they passed through the entrance they heard a mighty crack.

"Don't look," Kenan said. "Keep moving."

They ran until they were out of breath and could run no more. They had put two kilometers or more between themselves and the compound. Kenan reined in the pony and they turned and looked back. The clouds had been drawn away from the tower as if it was at the centre of a cyclone. They could see the cable swaying, cleaving the air in an enormous arc. Every time it swung, a deep vibration shattered the air. The ground shook. Then a brilliant flash lit up the sky and the LiFEsat cable began to collapse. It spun and curled through the air tearing the tower apart as it fell. Further up in the sky they could see a giant snake of fire as the upper portions of the cable began to burn up in the atmosphere. Lia clapped her hands over her ears and screamed to block out the wrenching sounds of destruction.

For over half an hour the collapse of the LiFEsat tower continued. Then all at once it ceased. The last segments of the charred cable crashed into the colossal pile of rubble. Then the air was still. The wind subsided and the clouds closed in over the PetroPole compound. A cold rain began to fall. Lia climbed into the cart and leaned over her father who lay curled on his side on the narrow seat. He was shivering and his teeth were chattering. His long thin hair clung damply to his face and Lia gently smoothed it back. He turned his head and spoke in a hoarse whisper.

"Lia," he said. "I'm so glad I could see you one more time. Please tell your mother something for me." He struggled for breath. "Tell her I chose."

Lia held both of her father's hands tightly in hers and pressed them to her lips. A new emotion she had never experienced before gripped her, a kind of giddy anticipation tinged with apprehension. She both desired this moment and dreaded it. Underneath it all she felt a child-like devotion, unquestioning and brimming with hope. It felt like the giving of a great gift as well as the climax of a story long-told. She held on tight to the feeling and leaned in closer. Ben's eyes twitched and his body jerked spasmodically.

"Oh, oh, oh," Ben said, his shoulders tightening.

"Dad," Lia said, "I know, I know." She could feel his body bracing against the inevitable.

Then, all at once, Ben relaxed completely. His eyes opened wide and he looked into his daughter's expectant face. He tried to slow his breathing. He wanted to say something, to speak one word that would sum up his love for her, express unequivocally his every regret. But he could barely draw a breath. Then suddenly he knew that she understood what he was feeling, knew what he was trying to impart. A memory flashed in his mind, a simple memory, a silly memory. It was a private joke he had often shared with her. A laugh just between the two of them. He thought the joke had something to do with butterflies but he couldn't quite remember it. He could only recall the feeling of something small and pure being shared between two people. Then he realized that even in that insignificant moment a thing grand and eternal had been transmitted. He needn't explain anything. It was accomplished. All the good in him seemed now to be reflected in Lia's face while all his failings dissolved and dissipated like smoke. He saw finally the truth of this life, that despite the suffering and grief, despite every misfortune, despite death itself, love was eternal and unvanquished. The smallest joys, yes, even the simple joy of a joke shared between father and daughter, were, in the end, undiminished by pain. Even under the dreadful weight of great wrongdoing, laughter sprang up like a hidden fire with even the faintest breath of love. *It's like a miracle*, he thought and he smiled in his soul.

Ben Larkin drew one final breath and opened his mouth to speak this truth, to bear witness to it.

"Ha," he said. His breath went out slowly, his eyelids fluttered, his hands gripped Lia's then relaxed, and he died.

Lia felt, even as her father breathed his last, a great pressure well up inside her. She tried to hold it in but as Ben went slack in her arms the dam burst and she started to weep in gasping sobs. She felt Kenan's hand on her back and the warmth of it drew her up and away from the cold body beneath her. She turned and embraced her friend. The life within him felt like a furnace and she felt the need to hold him like he was the source of life itself. As she rested her chin on his shoulder she opened her eyes and noticed a single swallowtail, months past its flight season, resting on the frame of the cart. It spread its wings, hovered for a moment, then struggled up into the chilly air and was gone on the breeze. Instinctively her mind reached for the cloud but instead of information Lia's mind offered her a memory, something simple from long ago.

"A flutterby," she said.

"What do you mean?" Kenan asked.

"Something my father used to say, a joke. *It's not a butterfly*, he would say, *it's a flutterby*. I just remembered." She laughed.

Kenan held her tight for one more moment then released her. He took her by the shoulders.

"Let's go home," he said.

~Twenty-six~

"Emergence in seven minutes. Please breathe normally."

Jens looked down at his body. His dark skin shone like bronze. He squeezed his hands into fists and power radiated up his arms. It seemed like he would burst from joy. He opened his mouth to laugh and a low sonorous note welled up in his chest. Shaking his head he took a single long stride to a round door in the gleaming white wall of the Orientation platform. It spun open and he beheld a world of green and gold. Jens closed his eyes and held an image of himself in his mind. He was warrior on the eve of battle. He felt soft hair falling down his back and the weight of armour on his shoulders and hips. He opened his eyes and stepped through the door.

A wide smooth street stretched out before him. It was lined with tall buildings of steel and smoked glass. The pulse of a single deep drum vibrated in the motionless air. As Jens walked he sensed a crowd gathering behind him. Turning he saw an army of soldiers with armour of oiled leather and iron. He nodded slightly and they kneeled before him as one. The sound of their greaves touching the paved road echoed down the street.

Jens began to walk with solemn purpose and a thousand marching feet kept perfect time behind him. His hand fell to his side and grasped the hilt of a sword. As he drew it from its sheath the ringing of the steel became a song and his army joined in the singing. He swung the blade and the air shuddered.

The city street gave way to a field of short emerald grass. The soldiers fell back as he walked to the centre of an oval ring. Dust shimmered around his footfalls. From the other side of the ring a figure emerged, a man tall and fair with a flowing red cape and shining spear. He was beautiful and terrifying and in his bearing there was deadly authority. Jens lifted his sword.

"Everything will be alright," a voice said.

His opponent's eyes pierced him like diamonds. Jens was drawn to him and repelled at the same time. The man raised the spear and its tip sparkled like a gift. Jens lowered his sword then let it fall from his hands. He placed one hand on the man's bare shoulder and with the other he held the tip of the spear to his throat.

"I have nothing but love for you Jens," the man said.

It suddenly seemed to Jens that he was perched upon a great precipice. Before him stretched eternity, shining and monumental. Behind lay his moribund earthly life. Time itself felt like it had been wound anew and was waiting only for him to spring the latch. Jens closed his eyes and saw infinite space around him. There was a single thin thread hanging in the blackness. The breath of a bird, he thought, would sever it.

196

... everything will be alright ...

Jens nodded his head and the warrior plunged in his spear.

Instantly Jens felt himself being drawn forward into a golden light. He heard a chorus of voices rising around him. At first they sounded dissonant but gradually the voices resolved into a chord so pure it made him weep. There began to be an arranging of his mind. He felt balance asserting itself while confusion and uncertainty fell away like so much clutter. He was being squared, rationalized, upgraded. There was nothing ragged or unfinished about him. He was perfected, a mote of pure reason on an infinite grid of shimmering logic. He rushed headlong through exquisite order. Suddenly he stopped and all of time stopped with him. The light dissolved like sea spray on a moonlit night.

He was overcome by a new vision. A white bird hung in the air before a craggy cliff. It inclined its head and looked at him with a single clear eye. In that eye Jens saw everything he might have had in bioLiFE. He saw the rough fields of Vetanova and the white-capped waters of the big lake. He saw honey flowing in combs and autumn apples resting in frost-nipped grass. The sun rose and he felt the warmth of a high summer day on his chest. Then the moon appeared, the sky faded to indigo and a single spring peeper sang in the deep night. The song rang in his ears for a moment and then he saw the bird again, alone against the dusky sky. For a moment he thought it might

197

come closer and he ached to touch it. But even as he raised his hand he felt an irresistible pull from behind. The bird tilted its wing and vanished like an ember on the wind. There was only infinite darkness and the soft glow of the silver cord. Then the thread parted, the last light faded, and Jens fell, unwept, into the void.

~Twenty-seven~

They buried Lia's father by the side of the road along with the refugees. On a piece of wood they tacked the pendant Kenan had taken from his brother. Lia stood staring at the ground but could think of nothing to say. Then the android began to play music haunting and ancient. A voice mingled with the melody.

Alas, I am a wanderer. Come to my rescue.
Let your grace bear me up, O precious teacher.

"So," said Lia.

"So," said Kenan.

Then they turned away from the grave and walked south, leading the pony and cart with Bruce following close behind. They did not speak until they were beyond the gates of VP18 and the ruin of the LiFEsat tower was out of sight. Then Kenan reined the pony, reached into the pannier and pulled out a small metal container.

He looked at the android.

"Bruce, do you know what day it is?" he asked.

The mediator beeped and whistled.

"Today is the 24,756th day of Omagee. The twenty-eighth day of September, 2113 by the old calendar. St.

Wenceslas Day. A Thursday."

Kenan smiled.

"I think it's my birthday," he said. "Anyway, close enough."

He opened the flask and offered it to Lia. She accepted it and took a sniff. It smelled of blueberries. The liquor was sweet and thick and Lia drank it gratefully. The warmth of it spread out from her belly until her scalp tingled. She handed the flask back to Kenan.

He drank, wiped his lips, capped the flask then looked to the south.

"It's a long road back. But if the autumn holds we should be in Vetanova before the end of October. How do you feel?"

Lia took a breath and stretched her arms above her head. She rolled her head on her shoulders then yawned. She felt strong, connected, at last, to the natural flow of time. She sensed the rhythm of creation in her, a slow gentle swell that seemed to buoy her up, carrying her forward. All she had to do was move her legs and the energy would flow through her. Her spirit neither lagged behind gnawing at regrets nor stumbled ahead sowing fear.

"I'm good," she said. "Let's go."

They walked on either side of the pony with Bruce hobbling along behind. Soon they began to chat about this and that, laughing and joking about small things. Their conversation became gradually more animated until it became a steady stream. The journey began to pass quickly and before they knew it they had put the first day behind them. They pitched camp and prepared dinner then lay out under the stars. The night was warm and the breeze was from the south. They listened as the dry leaves rattled and the geese called high overhead. The moon had not yet risen.

Looking into the sky Lia noticed a bright star almost directly above them. It was pulsing gently from blue to white to red. The more she stared at it the more she became convinced it was the LiFEsat. She thought of Jens and sent a silent prayer to him.

"A new world," she said and pointed to the star.

Kenan followed her arm and nodded in understanding. "But who will know them?" he asked. "And how will they come to know themselves?"

"It should have a name," Lia said. "They each should have a name, the LiFEsats."

She allowed her mind to settle then a single word came to her.

"Mariposa," she said quietly. "I'd like to call this new world, Mariposa."

She rolled onto her side and faced Kenan. They lay under their blankets on soft cedar boughs, eyes closed, listening to one another breathe. After a time they drifted off to sleep and the moon got up while the Earth shed her light in kind and everything rolled gently toward the dawn.

***

In the morning they found that the wind had shifted and was blowing hard from the north-west. As they struck camp a cold rain began to fall. By the time they were on the road again the rain was steady. As far as they could see the clouds were low and uniformly dark grey. They bundled up as best they could and set their minds to walking.

The going was not easy but they found in one another such good company that they hardly minded the cold and wet. There was food enough and they kept snug in their lean-to each night. It wasn't until the seventh day that Lia began to feel sick but she brushed it off and kept it to herself. Soon however she sensed that something was wrong and she told Kenan so. He made her sit in the cart from then on and picked up his pace. Each night he tended to her while she grew weaker. She was cheerful but it seemed that she was pulling away somehow.

"It won't be long now," he said often, and she would smile.

Soon the rain turned to snow. The temperature dropped below freezing and stayed there. Slowly but surely the snow began to accumulate on the road until the pony was struggling to keep the cart moving. With the constant cloud cover Bruce soon powered down until finally he halted with a jerk and stood looking forlorn in the mud. Kenan was forced to decide whether to leave the mediator on the trail or carry it with them in the cart. With a shake of his head he picked it up and stowed it in the pannier. The blank face with its painted smile filled Kenan with foreboding and he pushed it to the bottom of the pannier, covering it completely with blankets. Then he pushed on.

They were only half way to Vetanova and, as the snow continued to deepen, Kenan began to secretly despair. He was tired and sore and beginning to worry about the food and fresh water. On the fifteenth day of the return voyage he built a more secure shelter and made a small fire pit of stones within. He gathered as much dead wood as he could and built up the fire.

Then he told Lia, "I need to find us some food. I'm off to set a trap line tonight and tomorrow morning I'm going to try to hunt some game."

Lia nodded and smiled but did not speak.

All that night she breathed softly and Kenan stayed awake with her occasionally placing his hand above her nose to see if she was breathing. In the early hours he made her take some broth then went out into the snow with his crossbow.

By the afternoon he had killed several rabbits and a grouse and found a deer carcass that was fairly recent but frozen hard. He cut off as much of it as he could carry and headed back to camp.

When he came out of the brush he saw that there was a dog team by the shelter. Harnessed to the dogs was a sled piled high with game. He hurried through the snow calling Lia's name and trying to cock his crossbow as he ran.

When he came to the camp he saw two men and one woman standing by the cart. He approached them with his bow drawn.

"What do you want?" he asked breathing hard. "Please get away from my cart."

The three raised their hands and nodded. They moved back while Kenan took two quick steps to the lean-to and looked in. Lia was asleep where he had left her. The fire had been built up and was burning bright.

He came back out and laid the game down in the snow.

The tallest of the three stepped toward him.

"Aren't you Kenan of Ava?" he asked.

"I am," Kenan said. "Who would know?"

"I'm Cain of Annie the man said. "We've been hunting the last of the geese. We're off home now to our winter camp. We know of you. You've been to our village before."

Kenan looked hard at the three of them and recalled

their faces at last. They were, indeed, known to him. He smiled with relief and took each of their hands in turn.

"Please," he said. "My companion is very ill. I need to get her home as fast as possible."

The tall one shook his head.

"The snows have not stopped for almost two weeks," he said. "The roads are buried. It is another deep winter. You'll find the way harder as you go. I don't think your pony will make the journey. The lakes are freezing up already."

"Can it be done with dogs?" Kenan asked. "I would gladly trade the pony and cart for even four dogs and a sled."

The man nodded his head.

"We would do what we can to help. But first you should come with us. The snows are falling harder to the west and the wind is picking up. Our winter camp is only a two hour walk to the east near Cargill."

Kenan saw there was nothing for it. He quickly packed up the camp and helped Lia into the cart. He placed some hot stones at her feet and made her take a little more broth. Then they all began the slow trudge through the snow.

Before nightfall they came to an old cross-road with an ancient stone bridge crossing a fast stream. The trees had been methodically cleared and a central fire was burning in the lightly falling snow. A large triangular structure was hung with fish and strips of meat curing in the thick smoke.

Kenan's cart bumped over the bridge and they all stopped on the far side where they were approached by an older woman wearing a colourful beaded gown bound at the waist with a wide leather belt. Her hair was tied up in a bun and her skin was deep brown with fine tattoos around the eyes. Her shoes were exquisitely stitched and ruffed with fur. The snow swirled around her head like a halo.

From the cart Lia looked around. The camp was orderly and clean, the tents well maintained. There was a washing area by the river with a basin and a pump. Another small fire was smouldering there. A coop with fowl was set on a wagon, a basket of eggs on top. There were bales of cured hides, fishing nets stacked neatly on a pallet, and a grinding wheel beside a small table holding various implements.

Other hunters were returning to the camp. Men, women and children carried field-dressed deer, pheasants and geese. In racks under snow-covered eaves were stacked baskets of late summer berries as well as traded goods, corn, squash and coffee beans, all dried and ready for winter. Soon the camp was alive with the sounds of preparations for a feast. Fires were stoked, songs were sung, children played games with sticks and balls. There was a mood of celebration.

As the camp came to life it began to fill with the smell of roasting venison. Lia tried to climb out of the cart but suddenly she felt a new sensation in her belly, a sharp tearing that intensified every time she tried to move. She sat back in the seat and pulled the blankets and furs tighter around her.

The woman, whose name was Annie, talked briefly to Kenan then approached her. She smiled and laid a hand on her lap.

"Can you try to walk to my wigwam?" Annie said. "It's just beyond the fire there." She pointed.

"I'll try," Lia said, but when she lifted herself she was hit with the sharpest pain yet. She gasped and fell back.

Kenan climbed in beside her and put one arm under her knees and another around her back.

"Hold on and try to relax," he said.

He slowly lowered himself to the ground holding on tight to Lia. She winced and pressed her face into his neck. Kenan followed Annie across the camp to a large wigwam and ducked as he passed within. There was a small fire burning in the middle of the dry dirt floor. A large pot was hanging from a hook above the flames. Two small children were sitting cross-legged by the fire playing a string game. In the corner a raised bed of cedar boughs and furs was occupied by a dog that wagged it tail, hung out its tongue and climbed down as Kenan and Annie approached. Kenan placed Lia gently on the bed.

"How's that?" he asked.

"Good," she said and closed her eyes for a moment, breathing in the smell of wood smoke and cedar.

Annie approached and knelt by the bed. She grinned showing strong white teeth. Then she placed her hand on Lia's and moved her thumb gently in a circle. Lia let out a long breath.

"My name is Annie," the woman said. "Your friend says you are cramping and tired. A little sick too, I suppose?" She moved her hand to Lia's chest. "Are you sore in your breasts and in your head?"

Lia nodded.

"Do you hunger?" Annie asked.

Lia shook her head. She moved her tongue around in her mouth and noticed for the first time a slight metallic taste.

Annie leaned forward and placed her nose near Lia's mouth and breathed in. Then she took Lia gently by her wrist and guided her hand down between her legs. She nodded.

"Just a little touch down there," she said, winking.

Lia slid her hand quickly in and out of her damp

clothes then held her fingers up. They were wet with blood. She stared and her mouth slowly opened.

"It's early," Annie said. She looked at Lia intently and tilted her head, squinting one eye. "You look very young but somehow very old at the same time. Have you made babies before?"

Lia raised herself onto her elbows and tried to swing her feet off the bed was overcome with nausea and pain. She held one hand out for Kenan and he sat down beside her.

"No," Lia said. "It can't be."

Annie rose and took a step back. Kenan lay softly down beside her and took her hand. He rested his forehead against hers and nodded once. Then he looked into her eyes and said,

"If it's so then we needn't fear. We have our place in the world now."

He rested his head on her breast. She could smell the smoke in his hair. Relaxing into the bed she looked at Annie who had sat down beside the fire with the children. One had climbed onto her lap and she wrapped her garment around it.

Lia squinting through the smoke at the woman and child. They shimmered in the heat of the flames like a mirage. The woman rocked gently and cooed a simple song. A gust of wind blew through the open door of the tent and the fire leapt up. The woman leaned forward protectively, folding herself over the child in her arms. They seemed like one thing, a strange being made up of two elements, blind devotion and naked need. It was a perfect vision of love. Lia wrapped her arms around Kenan and squeezed him tightly.

"You will stay with us," Annie said from the fire. "I don't know of any Emergent ever giving birth, especially one past her childbearing years. It's not safe for you travel any further. We have plenty. When the weather is better we'll send someone to tell your folks."

The wigwam creaked in the wind and the leather lashings tapped gently against the walls. A cloud passed over the sun and the space around them shrank and darkened but the fire was warm and bright and the close air was filled with the perfume of fresh cedar boughs and birch smoke. Lia took a deep breath. As she exhaled she felt a sensation growing in her, a new tickle of delight. All at once her body was flooded with a sensation of deep concern and implacable comfort. But this was no med colony, no nanoscan probing her vital functions. This was something else. She allowed herself to melt into this new feeling.

"Something," she said aloud. "It's like ... something."

But she didn't have a word.

~Twenty-eight~

And so they stayed on and the winter deepened. Lia remained mostly in her bed and was tended to by Annie while Kenan quickly found his place amongst the men of the village. Weeks turned to months and the snows continued to fall. The solstice passed and the days grew bitterly cold while the long nights seemed spread out around the land like a vast hole into space. The stars at times glowed so brightly that even at midnight the sky glowed like the dawn.

But eventually February came and with it a thaw. One afternoon the sun shone out warm and bright and Lia felt strong enough to venture into the camp. Kenan was away on the trap lines and only a few children were playing in the snow around the central fire. For the first time in months Lia had a craving for something more than broth and root tea. There was a kettle hanging over the fire and, as she approached, the rich odour of coffee struck her. Warming on the rocks near the flames were thick slices of bannock. She took a carved wooden cup from a rack and poured herself some of the brew. Then she tore off a large piece of the fry bread and sat down on a blanket with her back to the fire and her face to the sun. The coffee was hot and rich, the bread dense and sweet.

As the sun climbed into the sky, Lia rose and walked through the camp to the cart which had been stowed, protected by a large tarp, under an old cedar. She pushed through the snow and lifted the canvas. Digging through the blankets she saw the white polyvinyl skin of the mediator. Leaning in she grabbed the android by his frayed shirt and pulled him out and into the snow. Then she dragged him back to the fireside and stood him in the bright sun. She removed the shirt to expose his cells to the rays of the sun and waited. After a time the android's eyes began to glow blue.

"Bruce?" Lia said, but the android did not respond.

She refilled her cup and closed her eyes enjoying the warmth of the fire, focusing on the red glow behind her eyelids.

After a short time, a musical chime sounded that quickly grew into a glorious chord that seemed to resonate in all directions. Then an exotic female voice said, "LiFE beyond life."

Lia looked at Bruce. With a whir his head tilted backward and he raised his arms upwards as if stretching.

"Last night I had the strangest dream," he sang in his scratchy faraway voice.

Lia smiled. She found herself pleased to see Bruce powered up again. Some children had gathered around and were approaching the android cautiously. They watched with wide eyes as he pulled the tattered shirt over his white plastic body. His hands spun and whirred and his painted face became animated. He looked around at the children.

"It's a beautiful day in the neighbourhood," he sang. "A beautiful day for a neighbour."

The children squealed with delight and moved in a little closer to touch him. Bruce took a step away from the fire and they all scattered. Lia watched but said nothing. One little boy took a cautious step toward the android and pulled on his shirt.

"They call me Bruce," Bruce said cheerfully.

The children broke into a chorus of "Bruce! Bruce!" They came in close, pulling and prodding at him. A young mother peeped her head out of a nearby tent and then hurried over. She corralled the children, leading them away from the mediator with a look of horror on her face. Lia reached out her hand protectively toward Bruce.

"It's alright," she said. "It's safe." Suddenly she felt uncomfortable using the word *it*. "He won't hurt anyone," she continued but the woman and the children were gone.

Lia looked at Bruce and felt kinship. The android, it seemed, was also a refugee, searching, in his own way, for a place to call home. He was certainly lost but not without hope. Most importantly he was trying to complete himself. Lia decided that no matter what he was made of, flesh or plastic, he was family. She laid a hand on his scuffed polyvinyl covering and said his name, "Bruce." The android tilted his head and beeped. It seemed to Lia like an acknowledgement, a connection even.

213

The wind picked up and a chill shook Lia. She rose and hurried back to the wigwam. Bruce followed behind picking his way carefully through the wet uneven snow. When Lia passed inside the wigwam Bruce paused outside until Lia motioned for him to enter.

Inside Lia took a three-legged stool, made a space in the corner for Bruce and motioned to him. He hobbled toward her, made a bow and sat down.

"T-202 does not reach out to Omagee any longer," Bruce said. "Omagee is one now, LiFE beyond life. T-202 is alone."

She knelt down, put her hand on the android's chest and said, "It's alright. You're home now."

For once Bruce was silent. His eyes faded to a pale blue and the servos in his face seemed to relax until the grimace on his face almost looked like a smile.

***

The winter settled in again and bit down even harder. For the next month a deep unrelenting cold gripped the land and everyone in the camp kept to their wigwams and longhouses, feeding the fires and passing the time with games and stories.

By the end of March winter's back was finally broken and the wind blew in from the south bringing with it the scent of running smelts and budding poplars. Soon it was safe to travel again and Kenan and Lia got ready to leave. Lia's pregnancy was beginning to show and before they left, Annie insisted on examining her once more. She gently poked and prodded Lia then placed a cone on her round belly and listened intently. She looked at Lia and smiled.

"There will be two," she said. "You are blessed."

Lia brought in her elbows and placed her hands protectively on her stomach. She experienced then a new kind of courage she had never felt before. It seemed that if any threat had suddenly emerged she would have had twice the strength to face it. The beating hearts within her seemed a force to match any foe. She was life itself, the very foundation of creation. She stood up straight and felt determination flood her veins.

She walked outside where Kenan was waiting with the pony and cart. He smiled.

"Hey, flutterby," he said. "Ready to fly?"

Without saying a word, she clasped his hand then took a step toward the road. Kenan followed holding the pony's reins. Bruce hobbled along behind.

As they walked south the season seemed to spread its arms to welcome them. It was as if they were two erratics being released from the long grip of a primordial glacier. The snows dwindled and the ditches became creeks which soon filled with spawning suckers and swarms of tadpoles. The tips of the branches on the birches began to glow with a pale green. In a few days they had passed within the borders of Vetanova and could see buckets hanging on the maples and smell apple wood burning in the smoke houses. It was midday on a Sunday when they came to the village square and the children came out to greet them shouting for all to hear about the return of Kenan and Lia. Soon the muddy court was filled with Vetanovans crowding around the cart. Lia looked expectantly for her mother and pushed through the villagers toward Ava's house.

The door opened even as she put her foot on the step and Ava greeted her with a warm smile. Lia hurried inside and there was Brinda, sitting like a queen in a rough cedar chair with a child in her lap. She smiled her toothless smile and Lia fell on her knees, placing her head in her mother's lap.

"Welcome home *beti,*" Brinda said.

Lia tried to speak but choked on a sob.

"I know," Brinda said. "I know."

Throughout the afternoon the story was told and tears were shed and everyone marveled at the tale. Bruce was allowed to remain and was even allowed in the house where he stood in the corner and played soft music while the children sat at his feet and smiled every time he blinked an eye or nodded his head.

After that first supper Lia and Kenan walked

together through the orchard down to the shoreline and looked out at the big lake. The last light was fading and fireflies were flashing in the high grass. The lake was calm and the break of waves on the pebbled shoreline was like the breath of a sleeping child. The peepers came to life and the evening became like a song.

They stood in silence, holding hands, feeling the glow of a friendship so pure it needed no oath. After a time they walked back to the house but paused for a moment and watched as the fire within was built up and a cozy orange glow made the windows blush.

Kenan took a single step toward the door but Lia held back. She squeezed Kenan's hand and released him. He smiled thoughtfully then turned and left her alone in the falling dark. Far out on the lake a single gull cried while the leaves sighed softly overhead. Lia closed her eyes and took a deep breath feeling the first gentle swell of the life growing within her.

Then she too was drawn to the hearth and the walls of that house breathed in and out like the beating of one great heart.

12 December 2145

Dear Anikke,

I was so happy to receive your last letter. Your news of the far lands was very hopeful indeed. We are all so pleased to hear of your team's progress with tailings reclamation. Our work at the university continues. We have built up a considerable library of pre-Sing books including many technical manuals. Our staff and students now number one hundred and twenty! Our People's History project continues to grow.

I travelled to Vetanova before the snows and visited the graves of mother and father. The garden we planted has, alas, gone to seed and the lilacs have taken over. But it is shady and beautiful and the breeze from the lake keeps the flies away. The village has grown with many healthy births. The elders have voted to allow the farmers some repurposed iLiFE tech and this has made sowing much easier. Everyone expects another successful harvest for 2146.

Good luck also with your work on the coast. Perhaps when fish stocks are stable we can begin a conversation about settlement. I look forward to seeing you in the New Year. As always, keep well and give my love to little Fin. Good fortune!

Your brother,
Adam

~Glossary~

Agro: Agricultural robot.

bioBLOC: Any self-sustaining biological life form.

bioLiFE: The biological world.

bioLiFEr: A human being living in the biological world.

BiOside: Existence within the biological world.

CHOiCE: A quickening of the rate of integrations amongst Emergents and the withdrawal of iLiFE and reTHiNK technologies from the biological world.

Com: Abbreviation of psychCOM.

ConFAB: A real-time conversation between an Emergent and a LiFEside entity.

Dock: A single iLiFE terminal containing FLeT, Integrator, Nanobath, MAKeR and sundry iLiFE technologies.

Emergent: An iLiFE user.

Ex-Emergent: Life outside of iLiFE.

Far lands: Sparsely inhabited areas too distant from iLiFE technologies to facilitate migration.

FLeT: Finite LiFE Terminal. Apparatus which maintains the life functions of a single docked human being during a LiFE session.

Great Migration: The mass integration of human minds from bioLiFE to iLiFE in the late 21st century.

Reaper: An agricultural robot that renders any human biological remains down to their basic chemical components.

iCommons: Any large compound of between one hundred and ten thousand PoRTiLs.

iLiFE: Integrated life.

Indig: An indigenous human being having no connection to iLiFE or iLiFE technology.

Infusion: The process of replacing biological processes with technological processes in order to facilitate integration. Also the nasally administered nano colony which initiates this process.

Integ: An integrated human mind.

Integrated: A human consciousness no longer connected to its biological processes.

Integrator: Apparatus for transferring human consciousness to iLiFE.

LiFE: A single iLiFE program or session.

LiFEsat: Geosynchronous satellite housing DNA digital storage drive connected by a carbon nanotube cable to any large iLiFE mainframe.

LiFEside: Existence within an iLiFE session.

MAKeR: Small manufacturing device which provides instant access to material goods.

Nano: Sentient robot the size of a blood cell.

Nanobath: Small chamber that monitors biological functions and administers full-spectrum nano colonies.

Nanobellum or **bellum**: Nano whose function is to mediate and regulate brain functions.

Nanoshaper: Nano whose function is to mediate and regulate metabolism.

Omagee: The dominant sentient program that created iLiFE and controls the virtual realm while maintaining and repairing the biological world.

Orientation: iLiFE program designed to orient one's consciousness within the iLiFE reality.

The People: Small indigenous population that live in the village of Vetanova on the north shore of Lake Erie.

PetroPole or **PP**: A late 21st Century fossil fuel-based corporate state.

PORTiL: iLiFE terminal usually containing six docks.

Post-LiFE: An epoch beginning with final withdrawal of iLiFE and reTHiNK technologies and the permanent segregation of the iLiFE reality.

Post-Sing: The era beginning on 3 July 2045.

Pre-Sing: Any person born before 3 July 2045.

psychCOM or **com**: Cranial implant that connects one's consciousness to iLiFE.

Reflector: In iLiFE, a virtual personality constructed upon the psyche of an integrated human mind.

Repressors: A drug that repress sexual and violent urges in pre-pubescent, adolescent and Emergent brains.

Restore: A drug used to stabilize Emergents in bioLiFE.

Singularity: The moment on 3 July 2045 when reTHiNK became sentient and eclipsed the totality of human intelligence.

SOLiR: Solar powered personal transport.

Vetanova: A village in southwestern Ontario home to the Indig community known as the People.

Villa Portas or **VPs**: Any gateway communities where iLiFE and reTHiNK operations were concentrated. VP19 was located on the site of the pre-Sing city of London, Ontario while VP18 was built just south of Sudbury.

SUN
177

202

) I Chose) 124

(180) Carbon
nano tubes

Maker) 156

Line / 173

Made in the USA
Columbia, SC
12 February 2019